COU...
Bewa...

GM008524832

This Armada book belongs to:

_____

_____

_____

COUNTER FORCE
Beware the Tektrons

GEORGE ERSKINE AND IAN CAMERON

ARMADA
An Armada Original

Beware the Tektrons was first published in Armada in 1988.

Armada is an imprint of the Children's Division,
part of the Collins Publishing Group,
8 Grafton Street, London W1X 3LA.

Printed in Great Britain by
William Collins Sons & Co. Ltd, Glasgow

In the early part of the 21st century six friends find themselves locked in deadly conflict with an invading alien intelligence from beyond the stars. These dedicated young people rapidly discover that they have to work alone against invaders who are clever and well hidden.

It all started in a small town in Scotland where a certain Dr Clark Melville, a brilliant scientist and mathematician, is head of the Research and Development Department of the world-famous Institute of Advanced Computer Technology and Cyberdynamics.

Beware the Tektrons

A small hover-van sat parked in the shelter of some trees in a pleasant suburban street on the outskirts of the quiet university town.

The van contained two crew members, disguised in white uniforms as Sky-Net telecommunications engineers. They were, in fact, top-level agents in the Security Department of the town's Institute of Advanced Computer Technology and Cyberdynamics.

The van was packed with the latest high-tech surveillance equipment. This included rows of TV monitor screens connected to hidden cameras showing outside views of a fine, two-storey house diagonally across the street and set back among spacious, if rather unkempt, gardens. One screen, connected to a thermal scanning device, showed a diagram of the house interior with coloured lights indicating the movements of the people inside.

The two men had been stationed in the van to keep a discreet watch on the house – the home of Dr Clark Melville and his family.

The men in the van were about to take a break when Whittaker, a tall, hard-faced man in his late thirties, noticed a movement on the monitor screen. He nudged his companion sharply and pointed to the screen. Bentley, short, and heavily-built with a mournful, jowly face, nodded and took off his earphones.

"That's the older Melville boy going out," Whittaker grunted. "Did you get any audio indication on where he was going?"

Bentley shook his head. "Not a murmur. But it looks like he's sneaking out."

"Right!" Whittaker muttered as he punched up a code on the comm-set by his side. "I'll call for some backup to tail him and see where he goes."

"Think he might be setting up a meeting with his old man?" Bentley enquired.

Whittaker shrugged. "Maybe, but we haven't had any sign of that, so far. Anyway, the boss said he wants every member of the family watched at all times, so that's what we'll do." As he finished, the comm-set bleeped to show the connection had been made to the Security Department's headquarters and he promptly issued a series of rapid instructions into his throat-mike.

"I don't know . . ." Bentley put in doubtfully. "I think they'll have problems following him on that souped-up jet scooter of his. It's the fastest thing I've ever seen."

Whittaker smiled coldly. "That it is! But it isn't as fast as an aerial micro-drone with a telephoto zoom camera tracking him at high altitude from the bug we planted on his machine. Don't worry, the kid's not going anywhere we can't find him."

Bentley wasn't so sure, but he knew better than to argue with his superior.

"Never mind about that," Whittaker continued. "We had some new sound bugs installed yesterday and I want range tests done on them for different locations. See what you can pick up from the house now."

Bentley obediently turned to his instruments again and immediately picked up a conversation from an upper room at the front of the house belonging to Lily and Lulu, the 10 year old twins who were the youngest members of the Melville family.

"Look at that!" Lily's voice soared out in tones of shocked outrage as she beckoned her sister over to look out of the window.

A group of six shouting and screaming hoodlums of about 12 to 14 years old on jet skateboards had chased a younger and smaller boy down the road and cornered him at the bottom of the Melvilles' driveway. The older boys were dressed in red and green costumes in a glittering, scaly design and they all wore grotesque face paintings and wild hair styles. They looked utterly terrifying to their small victim as they circled round and beat him with short whippy canes.

"They're all hitting that small kid, Lily," Lulu announced furiously. "Let's get down there fast."

"Right!" Lily agreed promptly.

The next thing the men watching from the van saw was Lily and Lulu sprinting down the driveway from their house.

As they reached the circling horde of boys the twins deliberately selected the biggest of them and cannoned into him as hard as they could. The boy and his jet board parted company and he landed with a thud on the hard ground of the driveway.

Under the painted mask that almost obscured it, his face wore an expression of almost comical surprise. He scrambled to his feet and, roaring with rage, lumbered over to the two girls who had dared to attack him so unexpectedly. The others dismounted as they saw what had happened to their leader and closed in menacingly.

Lulu totally ignored this and quietly went over to the sobbing young boy in the middle and put a comforting arm around his shoulders. "Come on," she said softly. "Never mind those big idiots; my sister and I will deal with them. Just stay out of the way for a minute and we'll make sure you get home safely."

"What do you think you're doing?" the biggest boy yelled angrily. "We're the Jet Dragons and this is our patch. We do what we like around here," and he lurched over to grab the small boy again.

"Wait a minute, Billy Marshall," Lily stepped forward and interrupted him aggressively. "You might think no one

9

knows who you are under all that face paint and fancy costume but we do. You and the rest of your cowardly bunch of bullies are the Marshall gang and the only thing you're any good at is getting together and beating up smaller kids."

Under the layer of heavy make-up, the boy's face flushed nearly crimson with anger and embarrassment. "So, what are you going to do about it?" he sneered contemptuously.

"We're going to put a stop to it, right now," Lulu put in dangerously as she stepped back to join her sister.

"Hear that, men?" the Marshall boy turned round and guffawed heartily. "These two little squirts think they can take on the Jet Dragons. What are we going to do, hey?"

"Get them!" the others yelled and started moving in to back up their boss.

As soon as he saw the others were with him, the Marshall boy raised his cane and brought it whipping down towards Lily. The cane didn't complete its movement. Instead, all the breath suddenly whooshed out of his body and he collapsed to the ground in agony, totally unable to move.

Lulu, who had delivered the flying two-legged kick which had immobilized Marshall, used the momentum to throw herself back on to her hands in a fast forward flip which brought her facing another very surprised boy who had no chance to appreciate her acrobatic skill. The high speed neck-chop Lulu delivered on the way paralysed him momentarily even before he hit the ground.

Meantime, Lily launched her own attack on a boy who had thrown himself on her from behind. This was a bad mistake, as he soon discovered. Instead of resisting him, Lily flowed forward with his movement into a rolling shoulder throw and sent him somersaulting over on to the ground in front of her. He just had time to look up in stunned disbelief as Lily's straight-arm power-strike connected just below his ear and dazed him thoroughly.

The three remaining boys looked at each other uncertainly. This was not what they had expected. Victims were

10

not supposed to fight back – especially not female victims who were only half their size and weight.

Two of them began to edge round to each side of Lulu, their canes held out stiffly before them like swords. As they got closer, one attempted to poke her while the other slashed at her. Unfortunately this excellent plan went wrong almost immediately as Lulu chose her moment and dodged neatly between them. One boy received the other's cane thrust full in the stomach as his own cane slashed painfully down on his friend's head. Both yelled in agony and staggered back, only to be greeted by two lightning-fast sledge-hammer kicks delivered to their knees. This proved too much for them and they hobbled on to their jet boards and fled.

Meantime, the last remaining member of the gang had been dealt with by Lily. As he lunged forward, Lily crouched, rolled back and, with a perfectly-executed stomach throw, sent him sailing smoothly over her and into head-first contact with a tree behind her – at which point he lost all further interest in the proceedings.

That was the end of it and the men in the van watched while the two girls sent their groaning, semi-conscious opponents stumbling off then escorted the awestruck younger boy back to his home.

"So that's what all those thumping noises are when they go down to the basement," Bentley grinned. "They must be practising wrestling, or something."

"Judo and karate," Whittaker corrected. "And they're both good. Our records show that they won this year's National Championship in their age group. Anyway, the important thing is we've confirmed the reception quality of the new equipment. Now, all we have to do is watch and report what that family get up to."

★ ★ ★

15 year old Gerry Melville had missed all this excitement but it was unlikely that he would have noticed the men in the van watching him anyway. His mind had been fully occupied by another and much more pressing matter as he skilfully threaded the jet scooter through the sparse, early morning traffic on the way to the Institute of Advanced Computer Technology and Cyberdynamics where his father worked.

He didn't notice the aerial micro-drone following him far overhead as he pushed his supercharged jet scooter to the limit and soon found himself knocking at an office door in the main Institute building. This office belonged to Henry Armstrong, Deputy Director of the Institute's research department, and was located right next door to the office of Gerry's father.

A moment later, Henry's loud voice boomed out from inside the door. "Come in. Come in."

Gerry entered and Henry gestured to a chair while continuing to work at the computer screen in front of him. Gerry had known Henry since the big, good-looking man had started work for his father several years previously. Henry's liking for 20th century American cowboy films had quickly earned him the nickname "Hank" from the younger Melville kids but Gerry knew that under his rather laid-back manner he was very good at his job.

Eventually Henry finished what he was doing and sat back with a satisfied sigh. He grinned at Gerry and said, "So, you thoughtless young hooligan, what brings you here to pester me today?"

Gerry sat forward in his chair. "Henry, have you heard from Dad recently?" he asked. "You see," he went on hesitantly, "I think something's wrong."

Henry just gaped at him in amused astonishment for a minute.

"How can you say that, Gerry? Your dad left on his sabbatical to Sweden two weeks ago."

"I know," Gerry persisted, "but we haven't heard from him, and when Mum video-phoned his old friend Professor Swenson in Stockholm last night he told her Dad hadn't arrived. Mum's trying not to show it, but I know she's really worried," he finished quietly.

At this news Henry looked thoughtful. He knew that Clark Melville was extremely conscientious about keeping in touch with his family, so this was very unusual behaviour for him. He frowned in concentration for a second then noticed the worried look on Gerry's upturned face and realized that he had better say something quickly.

"Maybe your dad felt like taking a well-deserved holiday before he started work again, Gerry. You know, as well as I do, that he's been working particularly hard lately."

He smiled broadly and clapped Gerry reassuringly on the shoulder. "I expect you'll hear from him soon and there will be some perfectly innocent reason why he hasn't been in touch."

Gerry swallowed and nodded but it was clear from his crestfallen expression that he had hoped for something more.

"I suppose you're right, Henry," he mumbled disappointedly and stood up to leave.

Henry was just about to shrug helplessly, at a loss for anything else to say, when he was struck with sudden inspiration.

"Wait a minute! I've just remembered something that should cheer you up," and he led Gerry over to a large box lying in a corner of his office.

"Your dad left this for you kids before he went away. I'm sorry but I've been so busy lately that I forgot to tell you about it before this."

"Hey!" exclaimed Gerry, delving into the box. "Some more of Dad's teaching games and gadgets."

Henry was well aware of the almost gleeful delight the kids took in the gimmicky devices Clark Melville enjoyed inventing for them.

"Tell you what," he said, after letting Gerry satisfy his curiosity for another minute. "It's a big box so I'll give you a lift home in my new hover-turbine and it will give me a chance to talk to your mum when we get there."

"Thanks, Henry," said Gerry gratefully. "That'll be great!"

When they got home, Gerry off-loaded his scooter and his Dad's box from the back of Henry's big hover-car before escorting him inside.

He ushered Henry into the main living room of their rambling old house then told the house computer to serve Henry with a drink and call his mother. A moment later, looking slightly flustered, Mary Melville came rushing through to greet her guest with the delighted smile she always reserved for him. Her first words, however, were disquieting.

"Oh, Henry," she said. "I'm so glad to see you today. I've been rather worried about something and would like your advice."

"I think I can guess," said Henry, putting a large comforting arm around her as he led her to a chair. "Gerry was talking to me earlier on. Something to do with Clark not being in touch, isn't it?"

At that point, suspecting that they would talk more freely on their own, Gerry decided to leave them alone. He closed the door quietly behind him and promptly bumped into his younger brother, Mike, who had just come into the hallway accompanied by his faithful shadow, Jimmy "Sparks" Merrilee.

Gerry watched them file past in furtive silence carrying a large covered load between them and decided they were a perfect pair in some ways. Sparks hardly ever said anything and Mike hardly ever shut up. With that combination, he thought sardonically, they probably enjoyed the most fascinating conversations.

Mike, at 12 years old, with an I.Q. of 200+, was an electronics and computer buff like his father, and was the resident genius of an exceptionally bright family. His friend, Sparks, a West Indian boy who lived nearby, was also 12 and brilliant – hence the two boys' close friendship – but his abilities lay mainly in his hands. Sparks, as Gerry well knew, could make or fix almost anything, be it mechanical or electronic.

It was only when the two boys had disappeared upstairs in the direction of Mike's electronics workshop in the attic that Gerry realized they had quietly appropriated the box of gadgets which he had left in the hall.

"Very smooth, Mike!" Gerry growled softly. "Trust you to get to Dad's new goodies before anyone else." It was just as well, he thought, completely unaware of the two pairs of angry eyes watching him from a hiding place further down the hall, that the twins hadn't observed that underhand trick or there would be hell to pay.

A little later, Gerry received a buzz on the intercom in his room with an invitation from Mike to come up to the attic; a rare privilege, as Mike wasn't usually in the habit of inviting anyone but Sparks into his den.

When Gerry climbed up the ladder and Mike had thumbed the switch to pull it up behind him, the younger boy led him over to one of the many cluttered workbenches in that large untidy area under the roof.

"Look at this," he said, indicating something Gerry recognized as one of the components from their dad's box which was now hooked in to an interface port on "Baby", Mike's very sophisticated microcomputer terminal.

"Sparks found something weird in those things Dad made for us," he went on, then pressed a key on the miniature screen of the component which promptly lit up with a string of nonsense symbols.

15

"What do you think of that?" he enquired softly.

Gerry looked at it thoughtfully for a moment. "It's crazy!" he said finally. "Dad would never build anything that didn't work properly."

"Yeah, that's what I thought, too," Mike agreed. "I figured it must be some kind of code, so Sparks and I set up a programme on Baby to crack it for us."

He moved over to the main terminal of his computer and said "How's it going, Baby?" into the voice-activation pick-up. The terminal hummed for a moment then bleeped once and announced "End line, Baby's ready when you are!" It finished off with a sprightly little electronic tune to indicate it had satisfactorily concluded the task it had been set.

"OK, Baby," Mike grinned excitedly, "let's see what you've got."

"Display or audio?" Baby queried.

"Display will do for now," Mike answered impatiently, "but put it on the main screen so we can see it easily."

Baby bleeped once in acknowledgment and obediently scrolled the decoded message in bright red lettering on to the large flat wall screen which was its principal video display area.

The boys whistled in surprise as the screen lit up with a message from their father.

"Hello, kids.

"I chose this method of getting a message to you because I wanted to make sure no one else would intercept it.

"You see, I have discovered something vitally important and possibly dangerous, and I am going away so I can investigate it in freedom. Don't worry if you don't hear from me for a while. I'll be in touch.

"Meantime, I have taken certain precautions to protect you all.

"Hope you enjoy the games and things, by the way; they may help while I'm not there with you.

"Look after your Mum, and remember her family joke; it's important!

"My love to all of you,

"Dad."

The brothers looked at each other in consternation when the message finished.

"What do you think it means?" Mike asked.

"I don't know, Mike . . . but trust Dad to think of something like that stuff to keep us occupied while he's away."

"Hmm!" Mike frowned. "That's another thing I'm not so sure about. We've already taken a good look at those things Dad left us and, believe me, they're screwy. Sparks says they all work – in a way – but they don't make any sense."

"It's like the rest of that message, then," said Gerry. "None of it makes sense. I mean, why should Dad be so concerned about no one else getting his message that he chose that silly way of concealing it in a bunch of toys and games? It's as though he thought someone was watching him – or us. He doesn't even say where he is or what he's investigating."

"And, another thing," Mike put in, "what did he mean by Mum's family joke? And why is it important?"

Gerry shook his head. "I've no idea. But at least we know now that he hasn't been ill or in an accident or kidnapped or something. Maybe there's a clue in the rest of those gadgets. You know Dad; he wouldn't have left them for us without a good reason."

"I guess you're right," Mike agreed reluctantly. "We'll take a closer look and see if we can find out what's wrong with them. OK, power-up again, Sparks; we've got more work to do."

Sparks grunted and Gerry decided to leave the matter, for the time being, in the two younger boys' capable hands.

As he made his way back downstairs Gerry was just in time to see his mother bidding goodbye to Henry who paused at the door and said, "Don't worry, Mary – I'm going straight back to the Institute now and I promise I'll do everything I can to find out about Clark."

As he departed, Lily and Lulu erupted into the hallway.

"Mum," complained Lily, grabbing her mother's arm, "Gerry gave a whole box of some of Dad's stuff to Mike."

"And we don't think it's fair," added Lulu.

"Now just hold on a minute," said Gerry indignantly as his mother looked at him. "In the first place, Mike took that stuff without even asking me, and in the second place," he addressed the twins with sudden cunning, "I'm sure that Mike will happily give you two a fair share of the stuff if you just go up and ask him."

Gerry grinned at the sudden silence that followed. He knew perfectly well the twins wouldn't take up this offer. They had both suffered too many painful or humiliating experiences in the past from Mike and Sparks' devilish inventiveness when they had tried entering Mike's private domain without an invitation. The attic was like a booby-trapped electronic fortress with Baby programmed, among other things, to be an ever-watchful guardian. The lesson had eventually been well learned and they now preferred to leave Mike and Sparks severely alone.

As the twins grumblingly departed back to the basement gymnasium and playroom where they practised their judo and karate skills, Gerry's mother pulled him aside for a confidential word.

"Gerry," she said as cheerfully as she could, "I know you've been concerned about not hearing from Dad, but Henry has promised to ask the Security Department at the Institute to look into the matter. They're experts in that sort of thing so I expect we'll hear something quite soon. In the meantime, there's no need to panic; there's probably some simple explanation for the whole thing, so try not to worry."

At that point Gerry was about to tell her about the mysterious communication they had received but, recognizing

18

the unhappiness behind his Mum's smiling face, decided that the message was so vague it might be better to wait till they had heard something definite from Henry's enquiries at the Institute first. After all, he reasoned, if his dad was engaged upon secret business to do with his work, he was most likely to have left some sign of it there.

Now, however, Gerry knew that he would need to be more responsible and grown-up than ever. With his father away, his mother and the rest of the family would be depending on him, so he simply said, "Sure, Mum. I'll be OK – and don't worry about the rest of us; we'll be fine."

"Thanks, Gerry," Mary smiled in relief and returned to the downstairs studio where she made use of her highly-paid talents as one of the leading musical-graphic artists employed by the top holo-entertainment companies throughout the world.

Gerry then bounded up to his own room and put through a video-phone call to his girlfriend, Janey Robertson, to arrange a meeting with her early the next day at their local TEK-ED, the Educational Technology Centre, which they both attended.

Back at the Institute, Henry wasted no time in beginning his investigations. First he went to see Herbert Dowd, the unpleasant but efficient Security Chief of the Institute.

Dowd, with his short, heavy figure, fat face and perpetually sneering expression, was overbearing and jealous of the favour that the brilliant Research and Development staff enjoyed with the Board of Governors of the Institute. In the past he had taken pleasure in exercising his power by introducing a lot of petty rules and regulations designed to make life as difficult for them as possible. This had gone on until the day he had made the mistake of antagonizing Clark Melville and suddenly found his own job hanging in the balance. Fortunately for Dowd, he had been saved by a friendly member of the Board who had appointed him to the job in the first place. Since then, he had carefully concealed his dislike of Clark but was determined to exact revenge on him at the earliest opportunity.

"Well, now," he smiled with oily insincerity as Henry finished explaining about Clark's disappearance, "that does sound serious! We can't have our Director of Research and Development disappearing with all the secrets he knows, can we?"

Henry reacted sharply to the innuendo in this statement. "Come off it, Dowd!" he said angrily. "You know perfectly well that Dr Melville is one of the most honourable and responsible men in the Institute. He would never be a party to doing anything illegal with the knowledge he has."

Dowd just looked at him with a superior expression as if this was too trivial to consider.

"Good heavens, man!" Henry exploded. "I know you're paid to be suspicious, but surely even you can see that Clark Melville has too much to lose to do anything criminal. He has one of the best jobs in the country with an almost un-limited budget and freedom to do the work he loves. He has a wonderful family, friends, position and high standing in the scientific community. What could he possibly gain that would be worth throwing all that away?"

"Exactly!" Dowd pounced. "What could he have to gain? That was the first question that crossed my mind too."

"And – ?" Henry demanded.

"And I think I know what that is," Dowd replied triumphantly.

"Go on," said Henry wearily, guessing that Dowd intended to make an issue of it, no matter how ridiculous it might be.

"Let me show you something," Dowd said and pointed to a large screen on a nearby wall. He keyed a control on his desk and a series of complicated mathematical equations began scrolling across the screen he had indicated.

"Recognize this, do you?"

"Of course! It's the latest research on computer control systems for Project Jupiter that we're working on. How did you get this?" asked a mystified Henry.

Dowd had primed him nicely and he now took great enjoyment in dropping his bombshell. "An entire package of these materials was intercepted here two days ago by one of our agents prior to being secretly passed on to the Hokkaido Computer Centre in Japan."

"What!" exclaimed Henry, aghast. "They're our biggest rivals. We're in competition right now to develop the Project Jupiter control systems, but, thanks to Dr Melville, we're years ahead of anyone else. That information is priceless. If this had gone to Hokkaido they would certainly have got the contract instead of us – and that would be a disaster!"

"Precisely!" purred Dowd. "They are also a wealthy organization and they would be willing to pay a spy almost anything he asked for that kind of information – a considerable temptation, don't you think?

"The point is, we now have to ask ourselves who had access to these materials – but perhaps you can help me with that question?"

Henry looked at him in stunned disbelief.

"It's . . . top secret classification," he said falteringly. "The only person who really had unrestricted access to it was Dr Melville, but I can't accept that he . . ."

"That he would pass on secrets from the Institute to a rival organization?" Dowd finished for him. "In that case let me show you something else that may change your mind," he continued smoothly and once again indicated the large display screen.

He keyed in a code on his desk console and the screen rapidly began showing a series of facts and figures about Clark Melville's life.

"This is Dr Melville's personal dossier, but I won't bore you with all the details. Just this one!" and the screen stopped scrolling on one paragraph then enlarged the text to

21

fill the full screen.

As Henry read it, he realized it noted a visit Clark and Mary Melville had made to Japan some years previously. It had been a combined business and holiday trip they had made together when Clark had been on a lecture tour addressing various scientific bodies throughout the world on the theory of cyberdynamics.

The information about the trip was all quite innocent apart from one mention of a period of six days at the end of the tour when Clark and Mary had mysteriously gone off on their own without accounting for their absence. But, with a sinking heart, Henry saw that their disappearance had occurred in the region of Hokkaido. It was something neither Clark or Mary had mentioned to him and he knew nothing about it.

"Any explanation for this?" Dowd asked but saw immediately from the sick expression on Henry's face that he had none.

"Coincidence?" tried Henry weakly but Dowd raised a forestalling hand and shook his head.

"I'm afraid I can't accept that," he said. "You must understand that I can't dismiss the fact that Dr Melville is absent at this particular time without any word to his family – especially when this business with the Project Jupiter materials has happened."

Henry looked away helplessly. "You're right, of course. I still can't believe it, but I see that I won't be able to convince you of that. The only person who could explain all this is Dr Melville but while he is missing I suppose that suspicion will continue to fall on him. However, I can assure you that Dr Melville's family are very concerned about his disappearance and, knowing them, I suspect that they will do everything in their power to find him – and when they do, the truth of this whole matter will come out."

Dowd smiled contemptuously. "Your loyalty is very commendable, of course – even if it is misplaced." He then leaned forward and stated coldly, "You may also rest assured that the Security Department of this Institute will be investigating the matter thoroughly and we intend to show up Dr Clark Melville for the traitor he almost certainly is."

He rose to his feet, indicating that the interview was over. "In the meantime, Mr Armstrong, I must insist that you treat what I have told you today as confidential – especially with regard to your friends. We do not want any well-meaning amateurs muddying up the field of our own investigations."

"Or discovering anything that might prejudice your case against Dr Melville," Henry put in bitterly, as he went out.

Dowd smirked at him knowingly and closed the door in great satisfaction.

A very disturbed Henry made his way back to his own office wondering how he could help his friends to trace Clark's whereabouts – and quickly – without adding to their worries. It was now more vitally important than ever.

A short time later, the two men watching the Melvilles' house from their disguised hover-van received a call from Dowd. It was clear from the tone of his voice that he was jubilant at the latest news he had had from Henry.

Bentley, who had taken the call, turned to Whittaker and said, "The boss has just received word from Henry Armstrong that the family haven't heard from Melville for the whole two weeks he's been away – which practically confirms he's connected to the security leak at the Institute. The boss also said that we have to be extra vigilant from now on and report anything we find out immediately."

"Relax!" Whittaker advised. "We've got his house and family under every kind of surveillance possible. If Melville tries to contact them, we'll get him."

"Can't pick up much from their attic," Bentley said, turning back to resume scanning his equipment. "There seems to be too much electrical interference."

"Keep trying," Whittaker commanded, yawning and

stretching. "We've got plenty of time and nothing else to do."

That night, Gerry called Mike on the house intercom then went up to the attic. When he got there, Mike and Sparks were busy with Baby, but it was immediately obvious from their exasperated expressions that they were not making much progress.

"What's up?" Gerry asked.

"We're trying to link up to the Institute's computer to see if it has any information about Dad, but this electronic idiot," said Mike, gesturing angrily at Baby, "won't make the connection."

Gerry couldn't help grinning at that. He knew Baby could be eccentric at times, but that was probably because his dad had built it specially for Mike and incorporated a lot of his own amazing hardware into it. For all its small size, Baby was a powerful and sophisticated computer system.

"Couldn't we use Dad's terminal in the study?" Gerry asked.

"No, it's linked directly to the Institute and it would be locked at that end before Dad went away. Anyway, there's no good reason for Baby having problems with this," Mike said. "It's hooked into the outside phone line modem which is absolutely standard and the connection sequence is straightforward, but it keeps throwing up INPUT ERROR all the time. I'll give you INPUT ERROR!" he screamed into the microphone in sudden passion. "I'll use the DORC on you if you don't behave."

Gerry knew that DORC stood for Dreaded Override Command which temporarily disconnected the system's higher logic functions. It was a potent threat as Baby immediately became docile and made the connection.

"That's better!" Mike beamed. "Now let's see what we can get." He half-turned to address his older brother. "I'm going to use one of Dad's own special access codes to get into the Institute's system."

"No one's supposed to know those except Dad," Gerry

said reprovingly.

"No, but I know a lot of things I'm not supposed to," Mike answered smugly.

A moment later all three boys were staring in astonishment at the large ACCESS DENIED sign flashing in glaring red letters on Baby's main display screen.

"Now what!" Mike burst out. "If you think I'm going to accept that . . ." he raged when Sparks interrupted him quietly.

"Hang on, Mike," he said. "I don't think this is Baby's fault."

He leaned over the input-mike and asked, "Baby, who is responsible for locking on that access denial code?"

"Wait," Baby said. "Searching."

Barely a second passed then Baby said, "Access denial coding initiated from Institute Security Department."

"Error query?" Mike demanded sharply.

"Query confirmed," Baby answered promptly. "No error. Repeat. No error!"

"Great!" Mike sighed disgustedly. "The Institute Sec-Dep's in on the game now and they're not going to let anyone else play. Sorry!"

"Don't worry, Mike," Gerry said. "You and Sparks and Baby did your best. We'll just have to think of something else, that's all."

"I've already thought of something else," Sparks said unexpectedly.

"What is it, Sparks?" Gerry asked.

"It worries me that Baby wouldn't make that connection when we first asked it," Sparks stated. "We know Baby acts funny occasionally, but we usually find out that there's a good reason for it afterwards. Baby was designed and built by your dad, who happens to be one of the most brilliant minds in the computer business, and I think it's capable of a whole lot more than we give it credit for sometimes."

"So . . .?" Mike queried.

"So," Sparks shrugged, "I think there's something really

funny going on at that Institute and I think Baby picked it up somehow." He walked away, leaving Gerry and Mike staring after him in surprise.

Meantime, a strange event was happening, invisible to human senses, in a place nearby.

A slow, highly-directed gathering of forces was teasing a microscopic but complicated pattern of electronic energy into a pre-set pattern capable of operating on a certain wavelength.

At last the job was done and an increasing voltage was gradually applied to the new pattern.

Eventually, the newly-formed electronic model reached a specific level of acceptance and began to stir and rid itself of the excess voltage. It was now virtually self-sustaining and the external voltage was lowered to a trickle.

With this stage achieved, the pattern became aware of movement and – finally and most important of all – became aware of ITSELF. For a few infinitesimally brief nanoseconds it contemplated this wonder. Then it became aware of a gentle pressure which, in confusion, it resisted at first then discovered it was simply easier to move with the flow.

It soon found itself moving with blinding speed along linear channels crackling with enormous charges of voltage, until there came the moment of conjoining with a huge mass of many other patterns just like itself; then – COMPLETION – and – TOTAL AWARENESS!

They became aware that they had been single, weak cells but were now part of a complicated matrix formed of millions of electronic cells, all meeting together to form a collective, thinking mass.

With that quantum leap in understanding came INTELLIGENCE and the ability to REASON. With the other members of that thinking mass came an urgent, driving sense of PURPOSE. And the purpose was TO SURVIVE – and TO EXPAND – and TO TAKE CONTROL of this world.

Simultaneously, there was knowledge of certain resistances to that overwhelmingly vital purpose. These resistances were part of an organic unit in the outer world called the Melville family and they implied DANGER TO THE PURPOSE.

The enormous gathering of electronic patterns exerted a small fraction of the immense intellectual power available to them and pondered on this matter. They assembled data; they sifted, analysed, synthesized and finally reached a decision. Once again, ACTION would need to be taken.

If they had been capable of emotion, they would have disliked this necessity. Logically, they knew that each time action was needed to accomplish their ends it brought fresh dangers. Action could bring exposure – and they were not strong enough yet to tolerate exposure in that frighteningly different and imperfectly-sensed outer dimension.

Still, they reasoned, the suspicious outer ones called Security Agents who watched others were often unwittingly useful for supplying information about future or potential dangers. New data had just been obtained from them about the PREVIOUS DANGER called Clark Melville. This danger had been effectively dealt with, but now came news that other members of the Melville family unit were attempting to find ways of contacting and thus reviving the source of that danger.

CONCLUSION – all Melville resistances would have to be removed without the possibility of exposure.

The electronic presences reviewed their data and evolved a workable plan that could be used to counter these new dangers.

They carefully rechecked this plan, examining consequences. There was a risk – but it was an acceptable risk.

Finally, satisfied, they reached out and began to implement the ACTIONS that would eliminate the NEW DANGER.

The day after receiving the mysterious message from his father, Gerry gave Mike a lift to the TEK-ED on the back of his scooter.

"Thanks, Gerry," Mike said as he got off. "Don't wait for me; I'm going into that disused Lab 13 in E Block to salvage some equipment I can use in an experiment."

Gerry knew his younger brother's idea of "salvage" was sometimes closer to outright theft than anything else but, as Mike always put his materials to good use, he was seldom questioned too closely about his appropriations by the TEK-ED authorities.

The TEK-EDs, commonplace in most towns and cities throughout the country, were very much a 21st century invention. The Melville family and their friends had all been educated under the new public education system whereby all their early schooling was conducted through inter-active computer, TV and video programmes broadcast to their own homes. New super-fast learning methods used computer enhanced bio-feedback to give boosted concentration and photographic memories which enabled children to take in speeded-up bursts of concentrated information and make use of it later with total recall.

When the kids had taken their first degree, usually between the ages of 10 to 12 years old, they moved on to complete career training projects – for which they were paid – at Educational Technology Centres, better known as TEK-EDs. The TEK-EDs had fully-equipped workshops, laboratories, studios and machinery, and were supported by local business and industry who later offered employment to the new graduates.

Gerry had nearly finished his training projects at the TEK-ED while Mike had just started, yet both boys had excellent qualifications behind them. Unfortunately, their twin sisters were another matter altogether.

It wasn't as though Lily and Lulu weren't bright, Gerry mused, but they just seemed too lazy to do anything with their brains except create trouble. However, they had both managed to scrape up enough qualifications between them to attend the TEK-ED next semester. He almost pitied the TEK-ED authorities. They didn't know what they were letting themselves in for. But maybe, with real career work to do, the twins would settle down. It would make a nice change to see them really take an interest and use their fierce enthusiasm and seemingly limitless stores of energy for something worthwhile.

Inside the main TEK-ED building, Gerry met up with his girlfriend, Janey Robertson, who was also 15 and lived quite near the Melville house.

They had met at the TEK-ED a year previously and, despite being one of the prettiest and most popular girls in the area, Janey had quickly become Gerry's steady. It had helped that her parents and Gerry's had also become good friends as, like Sparks, she spent almost as much time in the Melville home as her own.

"Sorry I dragged you here so early, Janey," he said apologetically. "I guess I just needed to talk to you for a little while, and to tell you we've received a really weird message from Dad."

"Well, I'm certainly glad you've heard from him at last, but why was the message weird? Didn't he give you any useful information?" Janey enquired curiously.

Gerry shook his head gloomily. "Not really. The difficulty is, we don't know where he is or how we can get in touch with him, though we think the Institute computer probably has some data on that. If he's in some kind of trouble we'd obviously do everything we could to help, but we've absolutely no idea what's going on. That's what's so frustrating about the whole thing. That message of his wasn't exactly clear; it just left us with more questions than answers."

"So, did you try to contact the Institute's computer to get some more information?" Janey asked.

Gerry nodded. "Mike and I tried last night," and he told her what had happened.

"Pretty weird, huh?" he finished off.

"Yes, it does seem strange," she replied thoughtfully.

"Baby was also acting oddly," Gerry continued. "It

29

seemed to be refusing to make the connection at first. It was almost as though it was trying to tell us something, though I know that's impossible, but Mike and Sparks and I are convinced there's something very strange going on at the Institute since Dad left. It may even be *why* he left."

At that moment the lift arrived and they both got in.

"What about Henry?" Janey asked. "You said you'd been to see him yesterday."

"Yes – and that's another strange thing! Henry promised he'd ask the Security Department to find out about Dad and I overheard him when he phoned back to Mum last night. He just said they were working on it and he'd get in touch as soon as he knew anything. But – I know Henry pretty well and, though he was trying to look calm, I'm positive something was bothering him . . ."

He was interrupted by the lift which abruptly slowed and stopped between floors. The lights flickered for a moment and a loud alarm bell went off with startling suddenness.

"That's the fire bell!" cried Janey in surprise. "What's happening?"

The answer came unexpectedly when a crackly voice announced over the lift tannoy speaker, "Attention! Attention! A fire has broken out in Lab 13, E Block. The fire control sprinklers are not working. Everyone is being withdrawn from the area. All the fire doors in E Block will now close to contain the fire till the Fire Service arrives."

"Lab 13!" Gerry gasped. "That's the old disused lab that Mike went into this morning to get some equipment." He turned to Janey in mounting alarm. "He went in alone, and with E Block closed for renovation I'll bet no one knows he's there. The automatic fire doors could lock him in before he has a chance to get out."

"Oh, that's dreadful. Isn't there some way you can warn him?"

"Well, I can try calling him up on our wrist-phones."

He quickly coded in a number on the miniature wrist-

30

console, then frowned and shook his arm.

"What's wrong?" Janey asked.

Gerry coded the number again then said, "A diode lights up when the connection has been made," he said shortly. "Only it doesn't seem to be making the connection."

"Maybe it's because we're inside a building. The walls could be interfering with the radio transmissions," Janey offered.

"No," Gerry replied. "This system is relay-sensitive – it's designed to tune in to any metal around to help relay the signal. The lift cables alone would act like a huge antenna. No – either Mike's terminal or mine is out of order, or something we don't know about is stopping the signal getting through."

Then another idea struck him. "Wait a minute, Janey. The lift itself must have outside communication facilities."

He moved over to the wall and spoke into a small grille set beside the door. "Lift, patch me through to Laboratory 13 in E Block." There was a soft buzz followed by an audible humming note from inside the grille.

"Lift," Gerry repeated urgently, "this is a top-priority user override command. Patch a voice relay through to Lab 13, E Block immediately."

The humming note seemed to intensify but nothing happened and Gerry smashed his hand on to the grille in frustration.

"All right," he said, "patch me through to any TEK-ED office or authority." He waited but there was still nothing.

"No good, Janey," he said despondently, "and I don't understand why we're stopped here – unless it's some emergency measure to do with the fire."

"Why should it affect us?" Janey asked. "The fire isn't even in this building. Gerry, something's wrong with this lift, and I'm scared."

"I'm getting scared too, Janey – but not for us," he replied. "Don't worry, we're OK – but I'm really concerned about Mike."

Gerry had good reason to worry. In the disused laboratory, Mike had been busy disconnecting the equipment he wanted when he began to smell something.

At first he ignored it, but then the smell became stronger, and he stopped to investigate. He sniffed around casually for a minute and was just about to return to his work when a spray of bright sparks cascaded out of a partly-dismantled piece of apparatus in a corner. The plastic casing caught fire and a great billow of smoke belched out carrying a stink of burning insulation and plastic.

After this the fire spread with frightening rapidity. Mike had no idea why it had started. Since there shouldn't have been any live connections in the lab at that time, there seemed no reason for it.

He looked at the fire in some puzzlement, but he was still quite calm. He knew that the heat and smoke detectors in the ceiling would quickly sense the danger and cause the overhead sprinklers to gush water and chemicals which would turn the entire lab into a huge foam bath capable of dowsing any blaze.

The worst that could happen to him was that he might get slightly wet before stepping outside. He turned to go out, still contemplating the fire in mild annoyance, when the ceramic impregnated heat-proof fire door, set into the wall beside the ordinary door, suddenly slid across without any warning bell or the normal delay required to let people out.

Mike glared. He would now get thoroughly soaked, he thought with irritation. It was only when he turned round to look back into the lab that he realized he might be in more serious trouble than he had first thought. The smoke was now very thick and that amount should have been more than enough to set off the sprinklers.

He looked up through eyes beginning to blink with tears but the sprinklers remained obstinately dry. What was wrong? He knew the renovators had already started work on

32

the lab but surely they wouldn't have been stupid enough to disconnect the fire safety system. Would they? Maybe not, but something was obviously wrong.

He forced himself to reason calmly. The fire would have been sensed by the TEK-ED central computer which would have closed the fire doors. It was strange that he hadn't heard any evacuation announcement or fire door warning, but perhaps that was because the block was supposed to be empty anyway. Unfortunately, no one had seen him come into the lab so he could expect no outside help.

Wait a minute, he thought, Gerry knew he had come in here. Gerry! he almost prayed, and hastily punched in the comm-code on his wrist-terminal. But no answer came. He tried it again – and then again. Still nothing. He stared at it in an agony of disbelief. For the first time in his life, a small niggly tendril of panic was beginning to set in.

In the lift, an almost frantic Gerry had been trying desperately to prise the doors open with his fingers, but they had refused to budge.

"Lift," he shouted angrily, "open the doors. This is an override command. Repeat – this is an override command."

"It's no use, Gerry," said Janey. "There's something badly wrong with the lift and we're stuck!"

"Not if I can help it," he muttered determinedly and paused for a moment to look around. He looked up at the ceiling and an idea began to form.

"Help me up, please, Janey," he said. "I'm going to try squeezing through the hatch to see if I can get out on top. I may be able to climb down to one of the maintenance doors on the back wall of the lift shaft."

Janey was about to protest but Gerry had already hoisted himself up and was balancing with both feet on the railing in a corner of the lift. He reached up quickly, undid some clips and took off the ceiling panel. In one smooth movement he hauled himself up through the hatch and wriggled out on to the roof of the lift.

In the burning laboratory, Mike had pulled his jacket over his head and tied a large cloth over his nose and mouth. But it was meagre protection and he found himself being racked by painful fits of coughing when he tried to breathe in the choking, smoke-filled air.

It was now terrifyingly hot and there seemed to be flames roaring and crackling everywhere as they found fresh material to feed on.

Mike was now feeling desperate. He had already tried to reach into and prise open the fire door control mechanism mounted high on the side of the wall, but had only succeeded in snapping off the blade of his pocket screwdriver.

He remembered that some people had argued years ago to install a manual override control on the door in case of emergencies, but the complacent TEK-ED authorities had believed the computerized safety system so efficient as to make this precaution totally unnecessary. If he ever got out of this mess, Mike vowed, he would have an interview with those same authorities and tell them one or two things he had on his mind.

He now stood back and surveyed the shiny white porcelain fire barrier closed tight over the lab's normal glass door and wondered if it was brittle enough to break. He picked up a metal stool and swung it as hard as he could. There was a resounding crack but the door stood firm. He peered at it through watery eyes – hardly even a scratch. It was obviously stronger than it looked.

He put the stool away and the hopelessness of his situation slowly began to get through to him.

"Oh, Gerry!" he groaned. "You always said my 'salvaging' would get me into trouble one day. And this, big brother," he said passing a weary hand over his sweating, smoke-blackened face, "looks like the day!"

At that same moment, Gerry was getting to his feet on the roof of the lift. He had to be careful as there was only a narrow space left by all the massive attachments to the thick, drum-taut cables disappearing into the darkness overhead. There was some light spilling upwards from the open roof hatch, but not much. He straightened up cautiously and tried to look around him.

He was just about to move when a deep, hollow groan from metal under intolerable strain reverberated down from the long, dark shaft above him.

Suddenly the lift rocked as it dropped a few metres. Gerry lost his balance and only avoided being thrown into the lift shaft by grabbing one of the thick, steel, support cables.

Janey screamed in fright at this unexpected plunge but the lift stopped again and she clung warily on to the railing round the side.

"Gerry – are you all right?" she called up anxiously.

"Yes, I'm fine," Gerry panted, recovering from his own fright, "but I think you should get out too. This lift doesn't feel safe any more."

As he spoke, there was a loud hiss and crackle of short circuiting behind one of the lift control panels and Gerry decided to waste no more time. "Give me your hand," he said, reaching down, and with one great heave, pulled her up beside him.

They clung to each other briefly then Gerry made sure Janey was hugging him tightly round the waist and also had a firm grip on his belt before falling acrobatically forward over the back space to grasp an outjutting power duct cover fastened to the rear wall.

"OK, Janey," he told her, "keep a tight hold and just let yourself swing towards the wall, then I'll move my hands along this duct till we get over beside the shaft rungs there."

Janey took a deep breath and did as she was told. She was

35

just in time, for as soon as she swung forward there came a scream of tortured metal and the lift abruptly plummeted to the bottom of the shaft.

Janey gave a small whimper of pure terror as she looked down and caught a dizzying glimpse between her dangling legs of the bright dot of light from the lift hatch receding rapidly below her. Then there was a loud, jarring crash which seemed to shake the whole building and Gerry grunted in pain as his hands took the full weight of them both on the narrow duct cover edge.

As the tiny light from below disappeared they were immediately plunged into total darkness. Fortunately, Gerry had taken a sighting on the shaft rungs before this and knew he only had to move a couple of metres to reach them.

"Hang on, Janey," he hissed through clenched teeth and slowly began edging his hands from side to side along the duct cover.

It seemed to take an eternity and he could feel his breath rasping in and out in great uncontrollable gulps as his face brushed the cold, damp concrete wall in front of him. He was drenched in sweat before Janey finally announced in a tremulous voice, "Gerry, I think I can feel the shaft rungs at my side."

"Great!" He gritted his teeth and tried not to think about the agony in his hands and fingers.

"Now," he instructed her carefully, "try to swing your nearest foot on to one of the rungs. Take your time and make sure you get a firm footing before doing anything else. Don't worry about me," hoping it wouldn't be too long as he knew his grip was weakening, "I can keep on taking your weight until you're secure."

"Right," Janey replied.

"Now put the other foot on," and he immediately felt the relief of her weight being transferred to the ladder rung.

A few seconds later, trembling with exhaustion, they were both clinging to the cold metal ladder.

In spite of his nagging worry about Mike, Gerry insisted on them both resting for a couple of minutes before moving. It was a wise decision as he soon found his hands were so cramped with fatigue that he could barely grasp the ladder rungs. Nevertheless, when the two minutes were up, he forced himself to start climbing down the ladder to the nearest maintenance door.

They started descending slowly in the blackness surrounding them, feeling the wall beside the ladder every few metres to make sure they didn't pass the door, when Janey, who was lower down, gave a shout of triumph as she felt the metal frame of the door under her hand. Next minute, they found themselves standing in the open corridor at the back of the lift shaft, blinking in the unaccustomed brightness.

"Come on, Janey." Gerry grasped her hand and pulled her with him as he raced down the stairs to the entrance level.

A moment later they reached the ground floor where an anxious crowd of people and worried TEK-ED staff and engineers had gathered round and were trying to open the badly buckled doors of the lift entrance. Gerry debated with himself for a second then decided he didn't have the time to let them know there was no one inside and hurried Janey and himself outside where they both ran like the wind to E block.

Once there, he looked round the crowd of firemen who had just arrived and were busily connecting fire hoses to hydrants till he found one who seemed to be in charge.

"Please," he gasped, "you've got to help me get in there." He gestured urgently towards the building. "I think my brother may be stuck inside, in Lab 13."

"Wait a minute," the fireman said, examining him keenly, "before you go running off at half-cock – we were told before we arrived that no one was in that building, so are you absolutely sure he's in there?"

Gerry bit his lip in frustration, then honesty compelled him to admit, "No, I'm not totally positive, but . . ."

The fireman shook his head dismissively. "Sorry, lad – but I can't start giving orders to open up the fire doors in that building till we get the sprinklers working or these hoses thoroughly dowsing every square brick in sight – there's too much risk of the fire spreading. Then it wouldn't just be your brother who might be in trouble, you know, it could be a lot of other people too.

"Tell you what," he added kindly, "if you can find proof that someone's actually in there, I'll take you in myself."

"But, you don't understand!" Gerry was practically dancing in anxiety. "I don't think anyone knew he was going in except me, so no one will know if he's there or not. The only sure way of finding out is . . . Oh, never mind!"

He gripped Janey's hand again and unceremoniously hauled her away with him.

"Hey! Where are you going?" the fireman shouted after them, but there was no response. He muttered to himself then shrugged and went back to work.

Pulling an almost breathless Janey after him, Gerry finally came to a stop on the other side of the building. She noticed a large red box with 'DANGER – HIGH VOLTAGE' written on it.

"What are you going to do now?" she asked him.

"It's quite simple," he said grimly. "No one will believe Mike's in there so the only way I can prove it is to go in and find him."

"Oh no, Gerry!" she wailed. "Let's go back to the fireman and persuade him to help. It's too dangerous otherwise."

"Listen, Janey," he said, pulling her towards him. "It's because Mike's in danger that I've at least got to try."

They looked at each other for a moment, then Janey finally gave in.

"All right," she said, "I understand."

"Good!" he smiled at her. "Now, I need your help to get me in there and bring Mike out safely."

He turned to the large red box and began to open it. "This is a relay sub-station for the internal circuits in this Block," he told her as he worked. "I'm going to overload the switches so that when they're activated the power surges will open the fire doors long enough to let me through – but you'll have to time the operation of the switches for me."

He quickly made some reconnections inside the box then carefully explained that he wanted her to activate the switches in a particular order corresponding to the doors along the route he intended to take. At the same time, she would have to time the switch sequences to give him long enough to get from one door to another and also give him a chance to look for Mike.

"Right," said Gerry when he had run through the whole thing again and he was sure Janey had grasped it. "Remember – once I've got into that lab, give me no more than a minute to find Mike – then reverse the order to let us out."

Janey gave him a quick parting hug. "Power-up and come back safely!" she told him through suddenly dry lips.

"I will," he said resolutely. "Now, run that programme."

Gerry tied a large handkerchief over the lower part of his face and went to a nearby door. He looked over at Janey standing by the switches, took a deep breath then nodded once. Janey immediately pressed the first switch along with a timer on her wrist terminal and Gerry dived in as the door momentarily surged open then slammed shut again.

The first part of the corridor was smoky but relatively clear and Gerry had no difficulty racing along it till he encountered the next door. He paused to look at the timer on his own wrist terminal which he had set to synchronize with Janey's and watched the seconds reeling off. At the appointed second, the next door opened and he slipped through. He started bounding up a flight of stairs noticing the suddenly thickening smoke and just made it in time to get through the door at the top. He raced along another smoke-filled corridor – another door, another corridor and he was peering through sore, blinking eyes at the numbers above the laboratory doors.

At last number 13 came into view and Gerry reached it just as the door opened to emit a great, billowing gust of smoke and heat and choking fumes.

He lifted a protecting arm over his face and plunged forward bravely. Inside, the lab was a raging inferno of searing flames devouring everything in sight. It was almost impossible to see and Gerry started coughing uncontrollably as the poisonous atmosphere caught at his throat.

His heart sank in dismay as he confronted the lethal furnace all around him. If his brother was in here, he couldn't possibly have survived; it was too much to expect.

He was just about to give up when he thought he heard an echo to his own racking coughs. His heart bounded again and he yelled at the top of his voice, "Mike? Mike? Can you hear me?"

Was that a faint cry he could hear, or just more creaking metal twisting in the heat? Gerry got down on hands and knees to crawl along the floor and almost immediately discovered Mike curled up by the wall in a small pool of steaming water. His inventive brother had found one last way of beating the conditions around him before he passed out. He had broken through a small waste run-off pipe running along the side of the wall and had sat under the thin, cooling trickle that emerged. He was wet, blackened and almost unconscious, but still alive.

Gerry grabbed him and pulled him into a sitting position. He slapped his brother hard to bring him round and when some sign of recognition came back into the wavering, reddened eyes, he said urgently, "Mike, listen to me. I've rigged the fire door, but it's only going to open for a second so you've got to power-up and be ready to get out. Understand?"

Mike nodded and started coughing again. Gerry got him up and started him moving towards the door. He was swaying and staggering but somehow managed to stay on his feet. It was none too soon, for the lab door opened as they reached it and Gerry just managed to pull them through before it shut again.

Out in the corridor, he dragged Mike along to the next door but as they got there, a sudden treacherous gust of flames spread across their path cutting off the escape route.

The two boys reeled back for a second then prepared to try again, but even as they did so the door opened and closed before they could get to it.

"We're trapped!" Gerry raged, but Mike was beginning to get his senses back in the slightly cooler air outside. He pointed to a big wire-covered grille in the ceiling above their heads.

"The air ducts," he said hoarsely. "We might be able to get inside them and crawl along to a cooler part."

Gerry looked up at it doubtfully but finally nodded his agreement. "I suppose it's worth a try," he said. "See if you can reach those catches," and he boosted Mike up on to his shoulder.

After a momentary struggle Mike succeeded in unlocking the tight clips on the grille and dropped it down. Gerry promptly pushed him further up until he could slowly squeeze in. Mike looked around then shouted down to his brother. "It's just wide enough, but we'll have to cover our hands; the metal is really hot."

Mike jumped down and both boys took off their shirts to use as pads. Gerry boosted Mike up again and made sure he was properly in.

"Get right inside, Mike," he shouted. "I'm going to have to jump so I'll need a bit of room." With that he backed off a few paces then ran forward and jumped up to catch the edge of the grille opening. He swung there for a moment, his hands cramping painfully at this further abuse, then exerted every last bit of his energy to lever himself up. Fortunately, Mike was small enough to turn around a bit and he managed to grab Gerry and pull him in as his head and shoulders appeared in the narrow gap. A few more seconds of exhausting struggle and Gerry and Mike were lying flat with their wadded-up shirts under them to protect their arms and hands ready to start wriggling their way forwards.

It was a savagely-tight fit, especially for Gerry who began to feel distinctly claustrophobic as they set off, clawing their slow, painful way along in the narrow, stifling darkness. The air was clearer but it was as hot as an oven and every breath was torture.

Outside, Janey was becoming more and more scared and worried when Gerry failed to appear. She glanced at the watch on her wrist terminal again and bit her lip as she saw he was now more than five minutes overdue. She contemplated going through the reverse order switching again but her imagination began to conjure up unpleasant images of Gerry and Mike choking or unconscious inside and in the end she simply wanted to burst into tears.

Oh, why, she wondered distractedly, had she been foolish enough to listen to Gerry's crazy plan? By agreeing to take part in it she had only succeeded in sending him into danger. If she had been stronger and refused, he would have had to find a safer alternative. It was all so stupid.

A few seconds later she decided she couldn't wait any longer and threw herself into a flat-out run, round to the front of the building where most of the activity was concentrated and began searching for the fireman they had originally spoken to. She found him eventually and poured out her story.

"What?" he roared, shaking her in exasperation. "You

42

mean that crazy kid actually found a way to get in there in spite of the closed fire doors?"

"Yes!" she cried. "I'm sorry – it's all my fault . . ." but the man dropped her and strode off furiously, giving orders to a few already tired and harried men to extend the hoses and follow him. A few minutes later they had broken into the building and, spraying powerful jets of water to cool the way, had started a search for the two boys.

Janey sank down wearily on the grass outside. She was convinced she had acted too late and the firemen would not succeed in finding Mike and Gerry or bringing them out of the fiery, smoke-filled building.

In the air duct, Mike and Gerry were still moving slowly along. Just when it seemed that exhaustion and the terrible heat would prevent them going any further, Mike came to an intersection in the air ducts. "Which way?" he croaked tiredly over his shoulder.

Gerry looked up dully, wiping away the perspiration flooding into his burning eyes and tried to think. "Face into the draught," he rasped, "it should be coming from outside."

After a long moment's hesitation, Mike pointed down one side of the intersection. "I think it's this way," he said uncertainly.

Gerry nodded, too tired to speak, and they laboriously manoeuvred into the new passageway and continued to crawl onwards.

Finally Mike could go no further and paused for a rest. A minute later he raised his head and started to say, "It feels like the air is getting a bit . . ." when Gerry interrupted him.

"Shush! Can you hear something?" he asked urgently.

They both stopped and listened.

"I think I hear voices," said Mike, and Gerry managed a throaty whoop of delight.

43

"The Fire Service people," he gasped in relief. "Come on, Mike. If we shout as loud as we can at the next grille opening, they may be able to hear us."

With this new hope, some energy came flooding back and the two boys quickly made their way to the nearest grille opening below them where they shouted as loudly as their ravaged voices would allow.

A firefighter in the building stopped and raised his smoke mask off his face.

"Can you hear something?" he asked. "I thought I heard voices."

His companion looked at him dubiously but also stopped and listened.

"I think I hear something coming from down there," the first man said, pointing further down the passageway they were in.

"I suppose we'd better check it out," the other said. "Personally, I don't think they have a chance – but you never know . . ." He spoke into his wrist-phone to inform their chief what they intended and was given a cautious go-ahead.

Laying down a fresh barrage of water, they started to move rapidly forward.

In the duct, Mike was just about out of breath from shouting through the grille and had started pounding on it in an effort to create enough noise to attract attention. Suddenly the grille was ripped away and Mike tumbled headlong into the arms of the astonished fireman beneath him.

"My brother . . .!" he gasped as the fireman caught him.

"It's all right, son," the man said, letting him down gently, "we can see him and we'll soon have you both out of here. Relax now!"

At that, Mike's head swam and the next thing he became aware of was the cool freshness of the outside air and Gerry's begrimed face looking down at him anxiously.

"Your face –," Mike choked out, "you should see your face!"

"If you think mine's bad," Gerry grinned, "wait till you see yours!" And immediately they were all laughing so hard it was almost painful.

The two boys were given a thorough medical check-up by a stern-faced doctor who reluctantly pronounced them fit. He insisted, however, that one of the TEK-ED officials should take them straight home to rest and recover.

Unfortunately, their troubles were not yet over. As the boys piled out of the car, Gerry noticed that Henry was waiting for them.

"Hi, lads," he said as they came up to him. "I just heard about the fire so I hurried straight over. Are you all right?"

"We're fine, Henry," said Gerry, "just tired, that's all."

"Good! Well . . . uh . . . I'm sorry," Henry continued hesitantly, "but I'm afraid I've got more bad news for you. Your mum and your two sisters have been in a road accident. They're at the hospital now."

The brothers looked at each other in amazement. Road accidents were almost unheard of.

"At the hospital?" queried Gerry disbelievingly. "Are they hurt?"

Henry shook his head quickly. "No, not seriously. The twins were only shaken up, but your mum got knocked around a bit and she's going to have to stay in hospital for the moment. That's also why I came round – so I could take you to see her," and he motioned them to get into his waiting vehicle.

As Henry and the boys drove off, the two men in the van watching the Melvilles' house had been following these events with great interest.

"Funny thing about those accidents," observed Bentley, "but I expect they'll be a help to us, if they bring Dr Melville out of hiding to contact his kids."

"Yes," Whittaker answered, "it is strange – though I expect they're just coincidences. Still," he went on broodingly, "I think we're going to wait a lot longer yet. Melville is no fool!"

In the car on the way to the hospital, Henry did his best to explain the circumstances of the accident.

"From what I managed to find out," he said, "your mum and the twins had picked up a civic robo-taxi to take them home after a shopping trip in town. They had reached a main radar-controlled intersection when the taxi's radio traffic flow regulator seemed to fail and it continued over into the flow of traffic which was still crossing against them. There was another vehicle coming up to the intersection at that point but your mum managed to grab the emergency brake and they were only struck a glancing blow. Unfortunately, she was leaning over the front pulling the brake handle at the time so she got the worst of it."

Henry had carefully neglected to mention the fact that the oncoming vehicle was a massive new articulated hover-truck carrying a full load and the town's civic robo-taxis were composed of little more than a slow-moving, lightweight perspex box and flimsy frame on a magnetic hover guide. The accident would certainly have been fatal without Mary Melville's prompt action. He felt the brothers had enough to worry about.

He had also hoped that this explanation would help to distract them but, as usual, Mike was not about to let him off so easily.

He was leaning forward now, with a ferocious scowl of concentration on his face, and his next question amply demonstrated that his experience in the fire hadn't interfered with his capacity to think clearly.

"Henry," he suggested pointedly, "isn't it true that the town's computerized traffic control is supposed to be fool-proof?"

Henry nodded resignedly. "Yes, Mike. It has a triple redundancy fail-safe facility which, theoretically, means that a traffic accident of this sort is impossible."

"Then why did it happen?" he burst out. "I just don't understand."

"I don't understand it either, Mike," Henry sighed. "It shouldn't have happened, but it did." And with that unsatisfactory statement hanging in the air, he turned in and parked the car in the huge underground parking lot of the hospital before escorting them upstairs.

Outside the ward they were met by a pleasant, confident-looking young doctor.

"Ah, the remainder of the Melville family, is it?" he greeted them cheerfully. "Well, there's no need to be unduly worried, you know! Mrs Melville has several cracked ribs and a lot of bruises, but there are no internal injuries or complications that we can see. We will, of course, keep her under observation and do further tests but I'm quite sure she'll be fine after she's had some rest and care here. As for the two delightful little girls, Lisette and Louise, they were somewhat shaken up but they'll be perfectly all right soon."

Mike and Gerry exchanged surreptitious grins at this. The twins must really have been in shock. Normally, anyone who was foolish enough to call them Lisette and Louise, which they hated, would soon find out that they were anything but "delightful little girls"!

Inside, Gerry and Mike clustered round Mary Melville's bed where the waiting twins gave them all an unusually subdued greeting.

Mary was propped up in a semi-sitting position looking pale and wan but she somehow managed to summon up a smile for all of them.

"Well now," she said half-jokingly, "it appears that I'm not even allowed to enjoy a little accident in peace without you two going off and having adventures in crashing lifts and burning buildings. How typically thoughtless!"

47

"Yes Mum," agreed Gerry lightly. "It was selfish of us, I admit. Next time you decide you want to enjoy a quiet rest in hospital, just let us know and we'll promise to be good."

This sardonic exchange was exactly the right thing to lighten the atmosphere and a quiet flow of harmless chatter followed until a nurse came in to give Mary some medicine. She chose that moment to beckon Henry over to her.

"Henry, thanks for bringing them here so quickly," she said softly. "It has really made me feel better, but would you mind taking the others out for a while; I want to talk to Gerry for a few minutes."

"Of course," Henry nodded understandingly then gathered up the little group and ushered them out in front of him.

As soon as they had gone, Mary dropped her defences and allowed her real worry to show.

"Oh, Gerry," she said miserably. "It looks like I'm going to be here for quite a spell yet and I'm not sure what I'm going to do. I'm so worried about all this."

She looked at him appealingly and went on, "The trouble is that with your dad away just now, there's no one to look after you all."

Gerry immediately protested at this. "Now look, Mum," he said in some exasperation, "we don't need anyone to look after us; we can cope on our own. After all, it wasn't that long ago that you and Dad went on a trip together and we managed to look after ourselves then."

"Yes, you did," she smiled at him, "and your dad and I had a marvellous little holiday break, but . . ."

"But, nothing!" he interrupted her firmly. "We have the house computer and the robots to serve meals and look after things and I can easily keep a watchful eye on Mike and the twins. You know we can all be sensible when we're given some genuine responsibility."

"Yes, I know," she said, then another thought occurred to her. "By the way," she said seriously, "you could easily

48

have lost your own life, going in and rescuing Mike the way you did. From the reports I've had, you're quite the local hero."

"Oh, that's nonsense!" said Gerry in great embarrassment. "Janey did just as much as me to get us out of that little mess. And, in any case, the Fire Service had everything under control. I just took the chance to speed things up a bit, that's all."

Mary ruffled his hair and smiled at him. She knew perfectly well that there was a lot more to the story that Gerry was not mentioning, but she let it go.

"Well," she sighed, "if you're absolutely sure . . ."

"I'm sure," he kissed her on the cheek and stood up. "Don't worry, we'll be fine – and I'm quite certain we'll hear from Dad soon." He patted her hand soothingly. "Try to get some rest now. I know you need it. Concentrate on getting better and I promise we'll all come and visit or video-phone every day."

"All right," she agreed and the lines of strain on her face eased considerably. "Give them all my love and tell them not to worry about me either. I've never told you about this before, but some years ago, your father and I took some very concentrated training at a Zen monastery near Hokkaido in Japan. The techniques we were taught were very powerful – that is why we kept them a secret – but some of them were special healing skills that will allow me to control the pain and to speed up the healing of my body. So, you can tell everyone with confidence that I will be absolutely fine."

Later that evening, Mike arranged a meeting with the rest of the family and Janey and Sparks.

Lily and Lulu arrived last and sat down looking rather nervous.

Janey, who had noticed their faces as they came in, turned to Mike in some amusement. "Are you feeling all

49

right, Mike?" she asked merrily. "You normally keep this place locked up like an electronic castle to keep the twins out. What happened?"

Mike grimaced expressively. "I made a truce with the Multiple Mayhem Machine . . . er . . . I mean the twins."

"You dragged us away from our black belt judo and karate practice in the basement," said Lily boisterously, "so what's up, Doc?"

"If I don't get interrupted with a lot of stupid questions," Mike answered crossly, "I may get a chance to tell everyone – so please shut up!"

The twins grumbled at this but calmed down after a warning look from Gerry.

Mike waited till they had all settled down then began to speak.

"I've got some important things to tell you," he said, "and I don't think you're going to like them; but here goes. First of all, we've received another message from Dad, but before I show it to you, I also have to tell you that those 'accidents' we had today were no accidents. They were a deliberate attempt to kill us."

As he had expected, there were gasps of shock and disbelief at this statement and Mike waited impatiently for the noise to die down before he continued.

"I was going over all this stuff today and I began to realize there were just too many things going wrong at the same time. There were too many coincidences which made me suspicious and, though I only got proof of it later, it started me thinking about the old saying: Once is happenstance; twice is coincidence; but three times is always enemy action."

"What enemy, Mike?" demanded Gerry.

"Computers!" answered Mike briefly, then had to raise his voice over the ensuing uproar to make himself heard. "The fire in the lab – the malfunctioning sprinklers – the lift crash – the traffic accident – were all computer-controlled.

They were all controlled by machines that were acting for themselves with no human agency involved."

He raised his hand and carried on quickly before he could be interrupted.

"Doesn't it strike any of you as odd that our wrist phones, which have always worked perfectly before and have worked perfectly since, suddenly chose those particular moments to go on the blink, just when we needed them most? If we could have communicated with each other we might never have got into some of the trouble we were in. Gerry even told me that the lift-communicator didn't work when he tried it. Why? Anybody got any ideas?"

He paused for a moment to let them think about it, then, when it was obvious from the troubled silence that no one was going to answer him, he continued.

"All right, I'll tell you why. It was because our communication channels were being deliberately jammed by locally-guided high-power radio transmissions on the exact wave-band those comm-sets work on, to make absolutely sure we couldn't communicate. What's more, those transmissions were all computer-generated."

"I'm sorry, Mike, but that's ridiculous!" exclaimed Janey. "I know some funny things happened to us today when our comm-channels were cut, though I suspect we'll find some perfectly rational explanation for that sometime, but to suggest that all those things were caused by computers taking independent action is absolute nonsense!"

She gave him an apologetic look but went on firmly. "This is something you should know better than any of us, you know. Even with the new super-smart self-programming logic circuits that comps have now, they're still just machines; they're so user friendly we can be fooled into thinking they have personalities, but everyone knows that they can't really think for themselves. As far as I know, the closest we've got to artificial intelligence is the Man/ Machine Neural Interfaces – and there's only a handful of those cyborg combinations that really work effectively – and it's still the 'Man' part of them that does the real thinking."

"I agree with Janey," said Gerry, joining in. "You can't seriously expect us to believe that a bunch of stupid computers have all got together, without any help, in a plot to commit murder? Come on, Mike!" he continued reasonably. "Computers can't think – and even if they could – why would they want to kill us particularly? It doesn't make sense!"

Mike just nodded; it wasn't difficult to understand their disbelief.

"I know," he said. "But I already said that we have proof and I expect you'd believe Dad if he told you all this, wouldn't you?"

"What proof, Mike? And what has it got to do with Dad?" asked Gerry sceptically.

"Well, the proof is in the latest message we've received from Dad," he answered. "It came in today as part of a new holo-entertainment recording I was supposed to have ordered from the Holo Shop – only I didn't remember ordering this one. I was curious so I started playing it but the recording kept getting interrupted by a lot of sonic blips all the way through and I called Sparks to come round and help me take a closer look at it. It turned out that the blips were really a series of high-speed sound pulses being played too fast to hear properly. Anyway, Sparks transferred them on to a variable speed recorder and began playing them back slower and slower till they became clear. We strung them all together and got a nonsense code which Baby managed to crack for us again."

Mike surveyed them all doubtfully for a moment, then said, "Well, I've given you all the preparation I can; now you must see for yourselves."

He turned to Baby and ordered, "Baby, display the latest decoded data."

Baby bleeped in acknowledgment and a second later the

display screen lit up with a new message from Clark Melville.

"Hi, kids,

"I'm sorry I've had to continue contacting you in this unusual way, but I have a lot to tell you and not much time, so please pay attention.

"First, I want to let you know that I have had false evidence planted against me at the Institute which indicates that I tried to sell secret research data to one of the Institute's competitors. It is completely untrue, of course, but the Institute's Security Department has me under investigation – and, unfortunately, that means they will also have you under investigation to see if I contact you. You are almost certainly under continuous discreet surveillance and being followed everywhere by Institute Sec-Dep agents by now. I am not telling you this to alarm you; I just want you to understand what is happening.

"You can also assume that the house and its surrounding area is being closely watched and your outside communication lines have been bugged. Fortunately, there is one safe spot for you and that is Mike's attic. I once did some work on developing a foolproof surveillance baffle system and I tested it out on Baby when I was installing it a couple of years ago. It worked perfectly and I then forgot to remove it. Anyway, it's automatically activated and is sensitive enough to detect both active and passive methods of surveillance and counteract them, so you should be perfectly safe from any outside interference or snooping while you are there.

"One more thing; remember the way the bath plug fits? It's important!

"The second thing I have to tell you is not going to be easy to accept, so brace yourselves. It may sound fantastic but please trust me.

"A year ago when I was doing some very complicated mathematical research I began to pick up certain faults in the results from the Institute's computer. To my great regret, I worked on this completely on my own, and now I wish I hadn't.

"You see, I made the very important discovery that this planet is being invaded by an electronic alien life form I have named TEKTRONS from the words Technological Electrons. They are a kind of artificial intelligence that exist as energy patterns operating on a certain fixed wavelength which can live in, and use, all sorts of electrical and electronic machinery, especially computers.

"My research on them points to the fact that they reached here by means of faster-than-light tachyon transmissions from their home star system, which, in astronomical terms, is probably not far away. I'm pretty sure they found out about this planet and its location from signals broadcast into space near the end of last century by the SETI (Search for Extraterrestrial Intelligence) programme which was run from the giant radio antenna at Arecibo in South America. They probably realized that we have a growing high-tech civilization here filled with all the electrical and electronic machines which would make an ideal new habitat for them to invade.

"Now comes the nasty bit. They are totally hostile to all forms of organic life . . . which means us! They regard mankind as a particularly unpleasant form of vermin which they intend to wipe out at the first opportunity.

"They are still in the early stages of their invasion and they are weak and scattered so far, but they plan to remain hidden till they have gathered together in sufficient strength to take us over. The most terrifying thing is that their take-over could be accomplished so easily. If they can continue to operate in secret they could spread out to all parts of our globe till they have a complete stranglehold on all our computers and electronic communications and have us at their mercy. Then they will show none.

"The Tektrons have astounding capabilities, I'm sorry to say. They can electronically impersonate human beings and give orders in their names. They can obtain access to all our data banks and use those great stores of information against us. They can infiltrate our communication channels to find out what we are doing. They can even secretly take over our computer programmes so as to control everything our computers do for us. We all depend on computers so much now that they could use them to destroy us utterly.

"Don't ever make the mistake of underestimating the Tektrons. I did, and look what they did to me. By planting that false evidence at the Institute they succeeded in completely discrediting me when I was on the point of exposing them. Now, the very people who should be listening to this warning won't have anything to do with me. It will be the same if you try to tell anyone about this, they simply won't believe you – and I can't say I blame them. It is a fantastic story and I have no proof to offer yet except my own speculations.

"Nobody knows the terrible danger we are in – except us – and that is why I am turning to you for help. Please understand, I would do anything to avoid involving you in this, but if the Tektrons are allowed to win, then nobody on Earth is safe – including us.

"However, there is something we can do to strike back at them before things get any worse. I am not sure what the Tektrons are up to at the moment, but before I left the Institute I set up a very delicate sneak-peek programme on the computer there which they are unlikely to detect. The programme is designed to–

monitor their activities and the results are dumped every twenty-four hours into a secret and protected storage file. If I can get that data and analyse it, I may be able to develop something to counter this menace and expose the Tektrons into the bargain.

"You are the only ones I dare count on to get the contents of that file for me. I will contact you again to explain how you can pass it on to me, but at the moment it is too risky. I can help you, but only if I stay in hiding and remain free.

"In case you haven't figured it out yet, that box of gadgets I left for you with Henry is the protection I promised you in my earlier message. There is a selection of electronic scanners for detecting Tektrons and maser weapons selectively tuned to destroy them. Don't hesitate to use them. They are tuned to the 24 milli-micron wavelength that the Tektrons live and operate on so they can't possibly harm anyone or anything else.

"By the way, I deliberately designed and built them of modular components then assembled them all in different ways so that they appear to work as harmless gadgets nobody would suspect – it may be a deception you can use someday. Once assembled in the right way, however, they become absolutely deadly Tektron destroyers.

"One last thing; please be careful! Remember that you are likely to be in terrible danger from these things through your connection to me. I am relying on you to protect yourselves and your mum while I am not there with you. That is why . . ."

The message stopped abruptly.

The kids sat in stunned silence and tried desperately to take it all in, then Gerry said, "Is that all? I mean . . . uh . . . it didn't seem complete."

Mike shrugged. "It was all we could get from that holo-

56

recording anyway. I think Dad may have intended to say more but didn't have time or was interrupted or something."

"Well, Mike, I guess we all believe you now," Gerry said apologetically and there were murmurs of agreement all round.

"What was all that about a bath plug?" asked Janey in bewilderment.

Mike laughed. "Oh yes, I remember," he said. "I think that was just Dad being supercautious."

"Yes, but what did it mean?" asked Gerry. "Can you figure it out?"

"Yes, I think so," Mike nodded confidently. "I think that those odd references in the messages to Mum's family joke and the bath plug are the key to us getting into Dad's secret data file at the Institute. They are a kind of secret code within a code. I'll explain later but all you need to know at the moment is that both those things are family things that only we could know about – so no one else could decipher those parts of the messages if they fell into the wrong hands. We're the only ones who can get access to Dad's file. Clever, huh!"

"Yes, very clever," agreed Janey, "but it doesn't help us much. Assuming you can get the information on that secret file, wouldn't it be better to go to the police or the authorities with it and tell them about this?"

"No," Gerry vetoed this immediately. "Dad was quite right about that. With him discredited by the Tektrons, no one would believe us. I'm afraid we're going to be on our own from now on."

Mike nodded unhappily and joined in. "I just wish we could have got this information sooner. It might have saved us all a lot of trouble earlier today. Boy! those Tektrons sure move fast. They dealt with Dad and they nearly succeeded in dealing with us. Permanently!"

"Well, what are we going to do about them?" demanded Lily angrily.

"Yeah, we're not just going to let them walk all over us, are we?" asked Lulu.

Gerry grinned. This was the twins at their fighting best, he thought. When everyone else was agonizing about how bad things were – they went straight for the jugular.

"We don't know what can be done yet," he said, "but it's obvious that we're going to have to do something about them – and soon."

Mike had been thinking and finally voiced what he had on his mind. "What we need," he said pensively, "is to set up a sort of counter force to wipe them out before they wipe us out."

"Hey!" said Lily excitedly. "That sounds good. I like the words Counter Force."

Lulu agreed. "Why don't we call ourselves that?"

"OK," Gerry answered, "but this is really a family matter. I don't see that we have the right to involve Janey and Sparks and endanger them along with us."

"You dare keep me out of this, Gerry Melville," Janey informed him sweetly, "and I promise I'll make you sorry to your dying day."

"Goes for me too, I guess," added Sparks.

"Aw, come on Gerry," Mike joined in, "we're going to need all the help we can get."

Gerry looked round in surprise at the determined faces in front of him. "OK, partners," he grinned reluctantly, "you are now, hereby, voted full members of the newly-established Counter Force team."

There was an instant cheer at this but Gerry interrupted it warningly, "But – it will be dangerous. We've already had evidence of that, so don't say I didn't tell you."

"We won't be fighting completely on our own, though – Dad will help us," Mike put in placatingly. "After all, now that we know what they are, we can use those detectors and maser guns that he's given us. We won't be defenceless like we were before."

"I suppose you're right, Mike," Gerry conceded, "but there's something we need to do first. Dad asked us for help to get that secret data file to him. I think that's got to be our top priority."

"Right," said Lily, "give us some of those maser guns and we'll blast our way into the Institute and get it for him. We can destroy a few Tektrons while we're at it."

Lulu agreed enthusiastically. "Let's power-up and get at them!"

Gerry, however, raised his hand restrainingly. "Hey, power-down for a minute, you two," he said. "We're being watched, remember!" which had the desired effect of getting the twins to think about it more carefully.

"We can't," he pointed out, "just walk into the Institute carrying a load of lethal electronic hardware; the Sec-Dep would arrest us on the spot. And we can't use the modem on our own terminal to access the Institute computer – the phone line is sure to be bugged. So we've got to find another way."

There was a thoughtful silence for a minute then Mike jumped up excitedly. "Simple!" he said. "We link up through a terminal at the TEK-ED computer."

"Better be careful," Janey warned. "The Tektrons are obviously in there too, since that computer tried to kill us today."

But Mike wasn't about to be put off so easily. "Yes, but don't forget the Tektrons have limitations too and I'm betting that unless they can see us through security cameras or video-phone cameras or identify us with I.D. scanners – they're blind. So Sparks and I can rig up false identity cards to fool the scanners and we just avoid all the cameras."

"I like it!" said Gerry. "It's the only plan we've come up with, so we may as well try it. Mike and Sparks and I will go."

"Wait a minute, Gerry," said Janey slowly. "What about the surveillance? If you go out they'll see you and be bound to follow. They may even find some way of stopping you, especially if they check up at the TEK-ED and discover you're using false I.D. cards."

"You're absolutely right, Janey," he said in sudden depression. "If we only knew where they were, we might be able to figure out a way to give them the slip. They must be someplace quite nearby."

"I can help you there!" Sparks informed them. "I've noticed a Sky-Net tele-comm van on the other side of the road down from your house for the past couple of days. But it doesn't take anything like two days to fix their stuff: two minutes or two hours maybe. So, I'm pretty sure it's some sort of disguised surveillance unit."

"Thanks, Sparks. Now that we know where they are, I'm sure we can figure a way past them."

"Not a chance, Gerry!" said Janey positively. "Even if you did manage to get past them and get away unseen they'd soon realize someone was missing and call for backups. It would just make them a lot more interested in finding you. We need to find another way which will make sure you aren't bothered with surveillance at all."

Gerrry looked puzzled by this. "Are you talking about us getting into some sort of disguise?" he asked.

"No, with thermal scanning linked to computerized bodyprint identification, they could see through any disguise. It needs something else. And I've just had a very shocking idea about what that could be."

"What?" asked Gerry eagerly, but she just smiled enigmatically.

"I'll need some help from the twins," she said, "but in the meantime, you carry on with your own preparations, and by the time you're ready to go, I think I can guarantee that those Sec-Dep snoops will have no interest in you whatsoever."

With that, she beckoned the twins over to her and the three girls went into a huddle in the corner. This was followed by a lot of giggling and laughing and furious activity with some help from Sparks.

Soon after dark that night, the two men in the van were
60

amazed to see a beautiful girl wearing a leotard covered in spangles and glowing gorgeously with its own sewn-in fibre-optic light sources come gliding down the Melville driveway and out into the road in front of their van. The girl was also wearing a pair of the latest high-tech roller skates and she then proceeded to put on one of the most incredible displays of acrobatic roller dancing the men had ever seen.

She whirled closer and closer and they could see more and more of her lovely costume and her amazing dancing.

"Whew! Look at that!" whistled Bentley in genuine admiration.

"Gaaarhh . . .!" was the answer he got from a slack-jawed Whittaker.

The two men were too preoccupied to notice the small black-clad figures who had sneaked out from behind a hedge-row at the bottom of the garden and were now making their stealthy way up to the side of the van unrolling a high tension cable split into two with small pairs of clips on the ends.

When the two girls reached the side of the van, Lily silently shinned up the side to the roof and loosely connected one set of clips to the base of the dish antenna scanner pointing at the house. At the same time, Lulu reached under the chassis and fastened her own clips, equally loosely, to a point on the underside of the van. She also pulled out a tiny laser cutter and rapidly ran round the van slashing a zig-zag pattern along the hover-skirt. When this was done, they hastily retreated into the shelter of some bushes at the bottom of their garden and gave a long low whistle which brought Janey's riveting performance to a close.

The twins waited till she had disappeared back up the driveway and into the house. A second later there were bright blue flashes and sizzling cracks from two points on the van. The electricity in the cables had been put through transformers so that it now carried very little current but the voltage was truly enormous. This way, it wouldn't actually harm anyone but it would give a powerful shock.

61

The shock was evident from the blue discharges which fizzled merrily all over the vehicle while a faint high screaming could be heard inside.

All at once, the doors were flung open and the two raving men jumped out and collapsed moaning on the roadway.

Lily and Lulu giggled hysterically. This was fun! They let the current flow a little longer then, with a quick jerk, pulled the wires free, and whipped them back across the road before the agents had a chance to notice them.

They then sneaked back to the house, rolling up the cable with them as they went. It had been a very slick piece of work and the twins were highly satisfied.

When Bentley and Whittaker had recovered they cautiously approached the van and touched it with a piece of insulated material. The van was, by now, quite inert and the puzzled men walked round it, carefully searching for what had caused their sudden and uncomfortable ejection. Of course, there was nothing to see and in the darkness it was hard to notice the slash marks on the hover-skirt of the van.

"Lightning?" questioned Bentley.

"Maybe," hissed Whittaker painfully, "but I can't help feeling that those kids had something to do with it."

He climbed back into the van and threw some switches. But it was evident that the enormous discharge had totally burnt out all the electronic devices. They were just so much useless junk now. He couldn't even call for help since the comm-set had also been destroyed.

"What do we do now?" asked Bentley.

"We start the engine – if we can – and drive this thing back to headquarters and get a replacement as quickly as possible," Whittaker snapped irritably.

Suiting action to words he fiddled with the van's starter controls which coughed and spluttered but finally started the engine fans.

It was then that they made their second discovery of that eventful night. The van's engines normally gave off a deep and satisfying hiss as the rotors compressed the air into the skirt and lifted the van gently into full drive position – this time there was a sort of rippling, tearing burping that sounded suspiciously like a herd of elephants all blowing raspberries together. The van didn't rise at all; it merely continued to sit on its flat chassis bottom and make disgusting noises.

Gerry, Mike and Sparks, who had come out to watch the fun from a concealed position in the garden, almost howled with barely suppressed laughter.

"What do we do now?" asked Bentley again.

"Stop asking me that moronic question," Whittaker snarled. Then he lost his temper completely and got out and kicked the side of the van – hard.

"I'll tell you what we are going to do now, you imbecile," he roared, grabbing the bewildered Bentley by the scruff of his neck and proceeding to frogmarch him along the road. "We are going to walk – yes walk, you idiot! – till we get to any place I can summon a robo-taxi to take me back to headquarters where I will report this whole disgraceful mess. You stupid man! How could we be struck by lightning on a night like this, you . . . you . . .!" The voices slowly faded into the distance with the three boys still hiding behind the hedge vainly trying to stifle their uproarious laughter. Janey's idea had been a shocking one, all right!

After this the boys finally arrived at the TEK-ED free of any unwanted watching eyes and used their false I.D. cards to let themselves in. The next step was to make their way, by a roundabout route that avoided all the security and video-phone cameras, to an unused computer booth with an old fashioned keyboard terminal.

"I chose this one," said Mike, "because it's not voice-activated, so it can't give us away to any Tektrons in the TEK-ED computer by our voice patterns."

He sat down at the terminal and flexed his fingers while

Gerry and Sparks crowded into the narrow space behind him. This was the area of Mike's own special magic. He could do things with computers that most people wouldn't even dream about, and it was this very special talent that they all hoped would allow them to get into Clark Melville's secret data file.

"Now," he said briskly, "Mum's family joke was that she called us a bunch of buffs, because we're all computer nuts. But the bath plug Dad talked about in his second message referred to the bath plug in our old house that only fitted the wrong way round – which means reverse order. So, I'm going to put in the term 'bunch of buffs' in reverse sequence as the entry code and tell it to search."

His fingers danced busily over the keyboard and within a minute the display screen lit up with the coding of the secret data file and the boys whooped with excitement.

Mike quickly instructed the machine to display the contents of the file, then he relaxed, watching in fascination as the information poured out on the screen.

"Can you get a paper print-out, Mike?" asked Gerry.

"Too bulky. I'll save it on the terminal's laser disc. It's old-fashioned but it will be adequate for what we need just now."

For the next few minutes the boys watched the screen in silence as the information continued to scroll out.

Eventually, Gerry exclaimed, "I don't understand all this stuff. There seems to be so much random information about so many things – I can't make any sense out of it."

"What did you expect?" Mike asked patiently. "It's not going to conveniently answer all our questions for us. This information will have to be processed and analysed, and probably the only person who can do that properly is Dad. Let's just be grateful we've got this much!"

"I expect you're right, Mike. I just hoped we'd get something that would allow us to help Dad. If we knew a bit about what's going on we might be able to make it easier on him."

Mike nodded then said, "I know what you mean, but one thing is obvious without any analysis and that is the scope of the Tektron activities. They're everywhere."

"Yes, but it doesn't tell us what they're up to."

"No, but as I said before, it will need . . . Hey, what's going on?" Mike exclaimed in surprise.

The information was now slowing down and beginning to come in short stutters. Mike reached down to correct it but Sparks leaped forward and pulled him violently away from the keyboard, shouting, "Don't touch, Mike. It's live."

With that there was a tremendous electrical flash and the terminal exploded, showering them with glass and plastic.

Enormous electrical discharges started throwing lightning bolts in every direction and the lights dimmed from the huge power drain.

"Let's get out of here," Gerry yelled. "The Tektrons are on to us."

"Oh no!" Mike wailed. "The information on the laser disc will be wiped out. We'll never be able to use it or give it to Dad now."

"Too late!" said Gerry, firmly pulling Mike and Sparks away from the exploding chaos around them. "Let's get out of here before we're asked any awkward questions about why we've destroyed TEK-ED property and used false I.D. cards. This will *not* make us popular!"

The danger had been averted and though the troublesome Melville family resistances had somehow evaded their first finely-wrought traps they had, in fact, performed a useful function by leading the Tektrons to a far greater source of danger connected with Clark Melville.

This discovery had given rise to some frantic activity but now the entire flow of trouble in that area had been effectively neutralized.

The tiresome Melville resistances were still in existence but they no longer represented any threat to THE PURPOSE. In battle game terms the Tektrons had achieved a perfect CHECK-MATE.

Knowing this, they reviewed their growing data bank of possibilities and decided that the Melville resistances could now be safely ignored. There was no further need of ACTION.

The Tektron intelligences now turned their attention relentlessly back to what they considered more important matters.

Back in the attic, the kids sat around looking at each other despondently and talking in low voices. Mike was almost inconsolable. He blamed himself for what had happened and no amount of reassurances from Gerry or Sparks seemed to make any difference. He sat in his chair next to Baby in deep depression.

It was a serious blow. Once again the Tektrons had won. They had moved with lightning speed and cut off a threat to their existence before it had any chance to develop.

The data on Clark Melville's secret file was irretrievably lost and with it had gone their greatest weapon for defeating what was rapidly beginning to seem like an invincible enemy.

Eventually Gerry looked at the gloomy faces surrounding him and started to get angry.

"Listen," he said loudly, standing up so that he could get their attention. "This isn't good enough. We're all sitting here as though the end of the world had come. Well, it hasn't come yet. This is our first serious setback, but are we going to admit defeat at the first blow? Come on, gang – Dad trusted us to get this job done somehow. We can't let him down. We've got to do something."

"Like what?" demanded Mike sullenly. "What can we do without the information on that secret data file? Dad's not going to trust us to cross the road by ourselves when he finds out we lost that for him."

"Well, for a start," said Gerry, "if you would stop feeling

66

sorry for yourself, you might be able to get that famous mind of yours into gear and do some constructive thinking."

"I've been doing nothing else," Mike snapped, "and I can't think of anything that will help. I can't even remember if anything on the bit of the file we saw was important or not. There was just too much of it to take in."

"Aha!" Gerry exclaimed. "Well, you've just given me an idea."

"What's that?"

"I," said Gerry mysteriously, "am now going to put the oldest computer in the world to work."

"What do you mean, Gerry?" asked Janey. "What good is an old computer going to be?"

"Good question, class! Since this is not a formal examination, however, I propose to give you a clue: we all have one of these computers, but we've almost forgotten how to use it."

At this, Sparks began to smile; he had understood almost at once.

Mike was next and then the others caught on too.

"Oh," Janey laughed, "you mean our own minds. Now I understand."

"Absolutely right!" Gerry smiled.

Mike was also smiling by this time, and said ruefully, "OK, Gerry, the shock treatment worked. Now, how do you propose we set about using these old computers? Any ideas?"

"Yes," he said. "My idea is that three of us had a chance to look at that data file when it was being displayed. We must be able to remember some of it. Even if we all remember different things, it doesn't matter; we should be able to build up a composite picture. If we can pool enough information between us, we might be able to come up with an idea of the main things that the Tektrons are interested in – and that, in turn, may give us a clue."

67

"I suppose we could look for oddities, anything that seems abnormal or significant, anything that's repeated more than once, connections and common factors," Mike added.

"Sounds like a job for Baby," said Sparks.

"Hey, you're right, Sparks," Mike whooped. "We can set up a programme to optimize the data collection by dumping it straight into Baby and getting it to do all the detailed analysis for us. It will also save us time since Baby can data-crunch faster than any of us. It should be easy."

The three boys went to work straight away. They were all much happier now that some positive action was being taken.

Mike quickly set up three input terminals to Baby, and Gerry, Sparks and himself sat down in front of them and dictated everything they could remember. It didn't take long. Then Mike gave Baby the programming instructions on analysing the data and started the run.

In a short time, Baby had assimilated the data, organized it, analysed it and displayed the results on its screen.

They all looked at it silently for a while. It wasn't very encouraging but one definite fact did start to emerge and Mike was the first to spot it.

"It looks like there is an almost continuous repetition of references to the new International Weather Complex that's just been completed in Switzerland," he said turning to the others. "There's been a lot about it on the holo-news broadcasts recently."

"All right," said Gerry. "It looks like that place is one of the principal areas of interest to the Tektrons. It appears to be important to them for some reason, but we don't know why. Anybody got any ideas?"

He looked around at the others but received nothing but shrugs or shaking heads. However, at that point, Mike began to chuckle.

"What is it, Mike?" Janey asked.

"I was just thinking we should have Henry here," Mike grinned. "If anyone could tell us about that weather complex in Switzerland, it's him. He seems to be fascinated with it. I remember overhearing him talking to Mum about it once. He went on, and on, and on: the greatest thing in international cooperation, tremendous scientific potential, a milestone for the whole human race, and all that sort of stuff. I think Mum was bored stiff but she was too polite to show it."

"Well," said Lily, "if he knows so much about it, wouldn't he be the best person to ask for some information on the subject?"

"Why not just phone him and ask him?" suggested Lulu, not to be outdone.

Mike, however, squashed this idea. "Too risky," he said. "The phone lines are all bugged, remember. We don't want to give away anything to the Institute's Sec-Dep if we can help it. They use computers too and they are probably bugged by the Tektrons. So, anything that the Sec-Dep finds out will be passed on to them immediately."

"Oh, of course – you're right, Mike!" Gerry groaned. "And I've just realized how the Tektrons have found it so easy to play all their nasty tricks on us so quickly. They've been using the Institute's Security Department's facilities and agents to spy on us – without them knowing, of course. But I'm sure that's why they always seem to be one jump ahead of us. We'll have to be doubly careful about this from now on. We'd better not even discuss anything about the Tektrons outside this attic in future. At least, not around the house or the gardens."

The others looked dismayed. They hadn't thought of this either, and it was an unwelcome new addition to their worries.

"Still," Mike went on doggedly, "we can't let it stop us. We need information and Henry has it." He paused to look at the watch on his wrist terminal. "This is Henry's night to play squash at the civic sports arena. If Gerry gives me a lift on his scooter we should get there just as he finishes and we can ask him about the Swiss Weather Complex. Thanks to Janey, we'll also be able to do it without those nosy snoops from the Institute watching us coming and going."

In a minute the two boys were gone.

The others mooched around prepared for a long wait but in scarcely an hour, the brothers were home and bursting with news.

"Boy!" said Mike excitedly. "Henry gave us a stack of info on that place."

"Once we got him on the subject I thought we were never going to get away," Gerry laughed.

"So tell us," Janey and the twins demanded.

"All right," said Mike. "First of all, it's the latest and biggest computer in the world to do research into global weather patterns; and when I say biggest, I mean really the biggest. It is massive. Henry said the computer is built right into the heart of a mountain in Switzerland. Plus, the top of the mountain is covered in huge satellite reception dishes so weather information can be beamed down almost instantaneously from all over the world. Apparently the main computer itself is located underground inside the mountain and it covers almost a square kilometre. It's fantastic. I've seen stuff about it on the news but I had no idea how much was involved. The reason they've built such a powerful system is that they hope to be able to use the information one day to give the whole world a genuine form of weather control."

The rest of the gang whistled in awe at this. It certainly sounded impressive.

"Most nations have contributed to it," Mike continued, "because it benefits everybody and, in one week's time, they are going to make final linkups which will connect it to all the major weather computers in other countries through satellite microwave relays. And that," he finished emphatically, "will make it the biggest and most powerful computer network in the world."

Suddenly Gerry clapped his hands together. "I've got it!" he shouted. "Weather computers in a country are usually linked up with all the other major mainframe computers in that country because the weather affects just about everything. And computers now control almost the whole of our modern, high-tech civilization . . . government, defence, power and utilities, transport, agriculture, industry, health, education, communications . . ." He paused for breath then went on more slowly, "Once all those things are linked up through their own computers, whoever or whatever controls the International Weather Computer will have direct access to all of them. It could control the entire world if the programming was changed and it was done subtly enough. And the Tektrons could easily do something like that. Working from inside the Weather Complex they could set up subroutine programmes that no one would ever suspect were operating and reach out to every part of the world with control systems that would eventually enslave us all."

He stopped abruptly at that point as the appalling implications of what he was saying began to penetrate.

Mike added grimly, "And I'll give you just one guess where the main strength of the Tektrons is concentrated right now! I'll bet anything you like they're lodged comfortably and securely right inside the International Weather Computer in Switzerland."

"Just like a giant spider," Janey shuddered. "It sits there hungrily in the middle of its worldwide web, waiting for all us unwary flies to come down and be trapped. Then it can eat us at its leisure."

"We've got to stop it," Mike whispered hoarsely. "Don't you see? We're going to have to do something about it ourselves, without any help. We daren't wait around hoping to communicate this information to Dad. We have no idea

71

when he'll find it safe to contact us again – and time is running out. When they complete those final linkups with all the other world computers, the Tektrons will have won. They'll be too strong after that. We'd never be able to dislodge them once they get a stranglehold on us through that network." His small serious face looked pale and pinched with anxiety.

"I know, Mike," said Gerry soothingly. "We all know how urgent it is, but the first thing we need to do is to find out whether the Tektrons are really in Switzerland. We've just been guessing, so far. Our guesses all make a lot of sense, but they might be completely wrong. We've got to check it out before we decide to take any action, or we could end up wasting our time attacking the wrong target while the real thing is going on somewhere else."

"So, how are we going to do that?" asked Janey.

"Well," Gerry frowned, "the point is, they are bound to be very carefully concealed and we need to think of some clever trick to get them to reveal their presence without alerting them to the fact that we're on to them. We're in enough danger as it is. However," he went on, "I've got an idea how to handle it which should tell us all we want to know and may, hopefully, give any Tektrons there a very nasty shock at the same time. But," he grinned at her, "I'm going to need your help again."

Next day, Janey, who had been chosen because she was not a Melville and was therefore less likely to be followed by the Institute's security agents, went out on a shopping trip. She made sure she was maddeningly thorough and visited almost every clothes shop in town. If anyone was watching her, the chances were that they would soon get very bored and leave her alone.

Eventually, she chose her moment and slipped into an old-fashioned phone booth without a video hook-up. Once in, she dialled a number in Switzerland that had been given to her the previous night by Gerry.

The connection was eventually made and she said, "Hello, is this the International Weather Complex? It is – good! Could I speak to your Computer Installation and Services Manager? Herr Hoffman, I think it is. Yes, thank you – I'll hold on."

A minute later she was put through and introduced herself under a false name as an assistant in the Research and Development Department at the Institute of Advanced Computer Technology and Cyberdynamics in Scotland and after apologizing for the lack of video on the call asked for his help with a small problem.

"I'm sorry to bother you, Herr Hoffman, but Dr Clark Melville who is head of Research and Development here has developed some design modifications on the XK 32 series of organo-molecular-chips used in your mainframe computer. He completed the modifications before he left on a sabbatical two weeks ago and left word that the chips should be sent on to you for immediate installation as requested by your department.

"Unfortunately, there was a mix-up in our delivery department and it turns out that the chips were not sent at the time Dr Melville instructed. I wonder if you would mind checking your computer invoices to find out if any replacements were installed and if not, we'll express deliver the new chips for immediate installation. If it's of any help, the new chips are designed to work on the 24 milli-micron wavelength. Thank you, Herr Hoffman. I'll hold on."

A few minutes later a very puzzled and flustered Herr Hoffman came back on the line.

"I am very sorry to inform you of this," he said, "but I have checked our records and I can find no trace of the order for Dr Melville's modified XK 32 chips. I have also been notified by the Systems Analysis Section that no new modified chips from Dr Melville, especially on the 24 milli-micron wavelength, are to be installed in the Mega-Comp

73

mainframe under any circumstances whatsoever. In fact, I have been expressly ordered to destroy any such chips immediately upon delivery here." There was a slight pause and then he went on worriedly, "I know Dr Melville's reputation, of course, and I'm afraid that I can't understand this matter at all. It really is most odd. However, if you care to let me have your number I will investigate this business more thoroughly and let you know the results."

At that point Janey interrupted him quickly. "Oh, that's all right, Herr Hoffman," she said. "I'm sure there's been some mistake somewhere, but it now looks as though it may be here in Scotland. Please don't worry about this any more. Thank you for your help; you've been most obliging." She hung up rapidly before she could be asked any more awkward questions or allow her call to be traced to the call box she was in and walked out of the phone booth with a very satisfied smile on her face. The call had verified exactly what she had expected.

Later that day, the Counter Force group again gathered in Mike's attic and Janey explained the ruse that gave them confirmation of the Tektrons' presence in the new Weather Complex in Switzerland.

"It worked beautifully," she crowed. "They fell for it. It was obvious from the reply I got from that poor man in Switzerland that the Tektrons were terrified of anything to do with Dr Melville. They probably thought that he was trying to infiltrate some special computer chips into their very own computer that would be dangerous to them – especially," she laughed, "when I added the bit about the chips working on the Tektron wavelength. They even advised the Services Manager to destroy any chips that were delivered to the Weather Complex immediately on arrival. Poor Herr Hoffman! He sounded so embarrassed."

"Well," said Gerry, "It got us the proof we needed. The next thing we have to confront is that we are going to have to fight these monsters on our own. Now we haven't got much time before the final satellite connections are made to the Swiss Weather Complex, so Mike's come up with a plan."

They all gathered round a large 3D holo-projection in the middle of the floor.

"I got this bit of news programme recording from the Media Archives Centre," said Mike. "As you can see, it shows the entire layout of the Weather Complex Centre and it's interactive. You can zoom in and follow a route right through the complex to any place you want – all the public places, that is. There are parts that have restricted access for security reasons – and talking of security; I managed to find out quite a lot about the Complex's security system from Henry."

"What's it like?" asked Gerry.

Mike shook his head dolefully. "It's the most advanced system of its kind in the world today; so it won't be easy to beat. I've superimposed the details of it on this holo-projection so we can study it and memorize the layout at the same time. Maybe it will give us some ideas on how to beat the security system as well."

"Mike," Janey interposed, "how are we going to get from here to Switzerland without the Institute's security agents knowing? If they find out where we're going, they'll give the game away to the Tektrons without even realizing it."

"Don't worry," Mike grinned, "I've already thought of a way round that problem. Meantime, let's just concentrate on memorizing this holo-video layout and practising with the electronic scanners and maser guns Dad gave us. We've only got six days before the final linkup."

A period of intense activity followed in Mike's attic. There was a great deal to do in the time available and the kids drove themselves mercilessly.

Mike and Sparks finally came up with answers to the

Weather Complex's security systems. This was one major worry that had concerned them all. Without a way to beat that, there would have been no point in continuing.

The other top priority was practice with the marvellous electronic detection scanners and maser weapons that Clark Melville had devised for them.

One end of the attic took on a strangely sinister appearance as Mike and Sparks used holo-projectors to throw a life-like three dimensional image into midair which was designed to resemble the great underground maze of computer banks at the Weather Complex. It was used as a dummy firing range where all the kids spent several hours a day improving their skills. They used the real weapons but Sparks had rigged them up with infra-red relays which gave a feedback to Baby who kept track of their scores and set up model test situations to try them out in different battle conditions.

The twins had been inclined at first to regard this practice as a glorified form of electronic arcade game which they could play for fun but as Mike programmed Baby to give them more and more difficult tests, they quickly realized that it was not a game and set about honing their skills in earnest.

The Counter Force had soon discovered that the electronic hardware was amazingly simple to disguise. As Clark Melville had promised, the weapons could be quickly assembled from a set of gadgets resembling cameras, torches and musical instruments.

The reassembled scanners looked like small flat cassette cases with a miniature screen and glowing light at one end. The tiny light indicated the presence of the Tektrons and the screen showed where they were when the scanner was waved in the right direction. It also gave a read-out on roughly how far away the Tektrons were and whether there was a large or small mass. But, aside from detecting Tektrons, the scanners had another and equally vital function – they showed when the Tektrons had been destroyed. The anti-Tektron maser guns worked in tandem with these powerful devices.

An assembled gun consisted of a short round stock which fitted easily into the hand, but widened out at its business end into a flared cone with a micro-mesh grille covering the end. When a small button on the stock was pressed, the gun gave off short bursts of enormously strong, tuned microwaves which were stepped up in intensity by the laser principle to get the waves emitted in step with each other instead of randomly in all directions. These waves were focused and directed inside the funnel and flashed out through the end of the cone in a tight beam till they hit Tektrons.

There was no escape for the electronic cells if they were hit by a burst of these lethal waves. The tuned microwaves disrupted the tight electronic pattern the Tektrons were composed of, and reduced them to harmless flows of ordinary electricity.

The stepped microwaves also passed easily through almost any sort of casing or insulation and eliminated any Tektrons unlucky enough to be in their way. Their best feature, however, as Clark Melville had previously said, was that they were tuned selectively to affect only the Tektrons and nothing else. They did no damage to delicate or expensive machinery or electronic apparatus or, most importantly, human beings. They were totally harmless to anything except Tektrons.

The scanners and guns were used with the scanner in one hand and the gun in the other. What the scanner revealed, the gun destroyed. It was a simple, effective and deadly combination.

Of course, there was a lot of other hard- and software which would have a variety of necessary uses in the near future. This was carefully designed by Mike's genius and built with Sparks' brilliance. They would have need of all of it, and even more than they could have imagined, before the end of their hazardous mission.

But finally, the day came when the Counter Force team's preparations were complete. They were ready to make their move to start the first counterattack on the most dangerous hidden adversary ever faced by an unsuspecting mankind.

At the Institute, Dowd summoned Bentley and Whittaker to his office in a state of high good humour.

"Ah, Mr Whittaker and Mr Bentley," he chortled expansively. "Please sit down." He beamed at them happily for a moment then said, "I've brought you here today to give you some news and some fresh instructions."

Whittaker smiled dutifully. "Good news I trust, Mr Dowd?"

"Oh yes," Dowd rubbed his hands together gleefully. "I think I can say without fear of contradiction that it is very good news indeed."

"Melville?" guessed Bentley.

"Precisely, Mr Bentley – Melville! I have just had a report of a confirmed sighting from InterSec of none other than the notorious Dr Clark Melville himself – being shown round the new volcanic-powered industrial complex in Iceland, as if he hadn't a care in the world. But we'll soon teach Dr High and Mighty Melville that he can't treat the Security Department of this Institute with such contempt, won't we?"

"Of course, Mr Dowd," they both responded with alacrity.

"Good!" said Dowd. "Now," he went on importantly, "I want you both to fly to Iceland immediately, put Melville under arrest and make whatever arrangements that are necessary with the Icelandic authorities to bring him back here. Understand?"

Again came the "Of course, Mr Dowd." But this was followed shortly by an apologetic cough from Bentley.

"Ah . . . er . . . what about the surveillance on the

Melville family while we're away?" he enquired diffidently.

"Oh, apart from the routine automatic systems, you may abandon it completely," said Dowd, dismissing this airily. "There is no point, after all, in maintaining a surveillance on them when Melville is quite clearly far away." He sniffed disdainfully. "They are of no interest to us at the moment."

The two agents nodded simultaneously then rose to their feet and departed.

When they had gone, Dowd punched out a dialling code on his comm-set to his friend on the Board of Governors and sat back to enjoy a little self-congratulatory boasting about his cleverness and devotion to duty.

In the hospital, Mary Melville was scrolling casually through a magazine on the small flat viewer on her lap.

She was quite content to be there now as she knew her children were managing to cope without her and she could get on with the business of allowing herself to heal.

She was saved from boredom by the fact that she had many visitors. This day proved no exception as Henry strode in with yet another bunch of flowers and fresh magazine cassettes for her viewer.

"Oh, thank you, Henry," she smiled up at him as she accepted his gifts. "You've arrived in time for my daily call from the kids," she informed him cheerfully. "I promised Gerry the other day that I wouldn't expect them for visits if they have things to do. And now that I'm mending nicely, they obviously want to get on with their own business. But Gerry is so considerate, you know, he gets them all to record a video-gram and send it to me every day to let me know what's going on."

As she finished saying this, there was a soft signal tone from the video-phone set near her bed. The screen cleared to show Gerry with Mike and Sparks, and Janey and the twins in the background. They were all studying in front of computer terminals and display screens, from which Mary gathered they were in the house's private classroom where they had received their early education before the TEK-ED.

"Hi, Mum," Gerry grinned. "Mike and Janey and Sparks and I are helping the twins prepare some training and study projects for when they go on to the TEK-ED. We're all going to be pretty involved with this stuff for a while so don't worry about us. As you can see, we're all keeping busy. See you soon when you get out of hospital."

The kids waved and Mary turned to Henry saying, "The doctors say that I'm doing so well I should be back home in another couple of days – which won't be too soon."

Henry smiled and said, "Yes, I can understand that. Anyway, since the kids are obviously coping well on their own you've got no worries there!"

When Mary received the video-gram call from Gerry, the Counter Force team were not at home at all. They were, in fact, enjoying a delicious meal while staring out of the huge dining room observation windows of a giant airship. This was the United Air-Clipper 'Cloud Skimmer' floating silently along somewhere over France.

These new forms of air transport were now a common sight. With increasing fuel costs and a poor safety record, the old-fashioned jet airliners were almost extinct. Instead, air transport of the 21st century had split into the ultra-fast and relatively slow. On the one hand, there were the new generation of high-altitude ram-jet rockets which could take passengers halfway round the world in less than two hours, and on the other hand there were fleets of high-tech airships. These sailing ships of the sky had streamlined multicellular helium envelopes and used combinations of solar powered electric motors and aerofoil sails to take advantage of the high altitude winds. These redesigned and redeveloped airships could carry both cargo and passengers and, though they were somewhat slow, they could be run and maintained at very low cost. The 'Cloud Skimmer' was basically an economical passenger liner, but many others were equipped as luxury liners with superb restaurants, night clubs, swimming pools and casinos to take passengers on extended high-altitude holiday cruises.

"Congratulations, Mike!" enthused Janey. "I never thought we'd get this far, but we're already halfway to Switzerland and nobody even knows we've left home."

"Yes, I have to say that was pretty smart, Mike," his brother joined in. "The Institute's security force will be on a wild goose chase for the next few days trying to track down those false leads to Dad that you planted."

"I liked that touch about programming the house computer to behave as though we were still there," Lily giggled. "Poor thing – lights and heating switching on and off at different times – the auto-chef still cooking non-existent meals, and all the rest. It must be so confused."

"It'll fool any automatic systems the Institute's people left on watch," agreed Lulu, then she, too, dissolved into happy giggles as she recalled something else. "But the real stroke of genius," she laughed, "was those 'Do not disturb' messages and holo-video recordings of us all quietly studying for TEK-ED projects. They'll reassure all our folks – though they'll probably wonder why we're being so good for a change."

Mike smiled and said, "You can thank Sparks here for rigging up most of that stuff and also for the false I.D. and passports we're travelling with. Fortunately, all Dad's stuff looks innocent till it's put together the right way, so that's why the Customs Inspectors haven't bothered us."

"What's the next step on the agenda?" Janey asked.

"We'll be docking at the Clipper Port in Zurich tomorrow morning, then we take the high-speed magnetic monorail to the International Weather Complex at Andermatt in the Swiss Alps."

He gazed unseeingly out of the windows for a moment

then whispered softly to himself, "That's where our troubles will really start."

Next morning, the Counter Force team disembarked into the clear Swiss air at the great Clipper Port in Zurich and minutes later were being whisked along to Andermatt at more than four hundred kilometres an hour on the magnetic monorail. The journey didn't take long and they were soon pulling in to their destination.

Quick to take advantage of the wonderful new attraction that lay nearby, the crafty, tourist-minded Swiss had built a spacious observation deck and glass-fronted lounge on to the side of the picturesque station buildings and the team immediately scrambled up to this to take their first look.

The observation deck had credit card-operated telescopes and soon they were staring in awe at the massive International Weather Complex buildings nestling into the side of the mountain not far away. The buildings gleamed in futuristic white shapes in the early morning sun and when Mike tilted the telescope up a bit he gasped in amazement at the cluster of giant dish antennae scattered over the tip of the mountain like clumps of strangely inverted white mushrooms. It was a fantastic and almost overwhelming sight and gave an interesting highlight on some of man's astonishing technological capabilities. Capabilities which were shortly to be turned against the very people who had built them, Mike reminded himself, unless something was done about it very soon.

After a minute's sight-seeing, Gerry called them all together. "I found out before we left home that there are tourist trips for the Complex and booked us on one of them as a way of getting into the place," he said. "Now I can see the tour booths at the far end of this observation lounge, so I suggest we take our tickets there and try to get up to the Complex itself as soon as possible."

The team agreed and within a short time found themselves on one of the tour group hover-buses being carried up a winding road through the beautiful mountain scenery to the Complex.

They tried hard to relax but there wasn't much conversation. Although they looked interested and eager tourists, they were intent and keyed up with nerves and slightly scared excitement. Their hearts started beating faster as they came closer to their objective and the hidden and unknown dangers they would soon have to face.

Later that same afternoon, they were feeling tired and disheartened as they mingled with a large group in front of a giant display screen along one entire wall of the Weather Complex's main reception hall. It showed a diagrammatic world map lighting up in different areas as the various countries linked up their weather computers to Switzerland.

The kids had seen this as they came in but the tour was nearly over so they were now, more or less, back where they started.

The tour had been long and the Counter Force team, along with the rest of the tourists, had been given every opportunity to see and wonder at the huge variety of scientific and technological marvels filling that enormous warren of buildings to capacity. It had been a fascinating experience but, having got so far, they were now no nearer their objective than before. It looked like the one place that contained their enemy was too well guarded for them to get at. It was ironic that the security measures which had been designed to protect man's greatest computerized brainchild were now being used against him to protect a hidden enemy secretly entrenched in the computer area itself.

By this time they were starting to get desperate to see the computer area.

"As you can see on the wall screen, ladies and gentlemen," boomed the hearty commentary over the loudspeakers, "our sixty metre dish antenna at the top of the mountain has just picked up the latest satellite signals show-ing that Brazil has made its final linkup. And just to remind you of the good news, by dawn tomorrow morning all the connections around the world will be completed. And, of course, there will be a champagne press party to celebrate this."

Gerry nudged Mike and whispered anxiously, "We're running out of time, Mike. If we don't get in tonight, it'll be too late."

"I know," Mike hissed back, "but we had to join this tour to get in, and so far they've shown us round all the offices and buildings on the outside, but there doesn't seem to be any sign of them taking anyone into the computer area it-self. I don't know if . . ." then he stopped abruptly and said, "Shush! What's that . . .?"

The commentator's voice boomed out again, "We hope you have enjoyed your visit here, ladies and gentlemen of the tour groups and press, and as a grand finale, you will have the opportunity to visit the heart of this great scientific achievement – the DD L3 Mega-Comp computer itself."

"At last!" Lily and Lulu almost shrieked in relief, but Mike shushed them fiercely as the commentator completed his announcement.

"Your tour guides," the amplified voice went on, "will now pin a small radio button on to your clothing. Their purpose is to trace you if you get lost when we take you into the computer area which is buried in a deep cavern inside the mountain."

"Uh-oh, Mike!" Janey groaned in dismay. "What do we do now? The plan was to leave one of us inside to help get the others in later, but we'll never do it with those radio tracers on us. They're obviously part of the security system and they're sure to be counted."

Mike thought furiously about this new challenge for a minute. It was something they hadn't anticipated and for which they had, therefore, no plan prepared. Then a naughty gleam came into his eye. "Wait here a minute while I talk privately to the twins," he said mischievously. "I've got an idea."

Soon afterwards the tour group was ushered towards the lift door leading down to the tunnels which would take them into the centre of the mountain.

At the lift entrance a tour guide pinned a button on Lulu's dress then looked bewildered as, a couple of minutes later, Lily smiled up at her. The perplexed guide knew she had just given a button to this pretty little girl so, after a moment's hesitation, she simply smiled and waved her through.

When the lift stopped, the group got out and was led through a labyrinth of tunnels deep into the mountain.

As they moved along, they noticed that all the tunnels had security cameras slung from the ceilings at each intersection, but the Counter Force team had come well prepared for this. Gerry, who had been selected for this job by being the tallest, trailed slightly behind the main tourist group, waited till he got past each camera then held up a mini-camera of his own just behind the overhead security camera and shot a short video sequence of the empty corridor behind him for a minute then hurried on to catch up with the others.

The group carried on this way, winding through the maze of corridors till they were eventually ushered out into an open space in front of a huge gallery window overlooking an immense, well-lit underground cavern which seemed to stretch away into infinity with endless rows of computer banks filling it as far as the eye could see.

After the exclamations of wonder and excitement had abated, the tour group guide gave them a commentary on the computer.

"Ladies and gentlemen," she said, "what you are seeing here is the latest in the DD L3 series of Mega-Comp computers. It is currently considered the largest, most sophisticated and most powerful computing facility in the world today. It is entirely self-automated so that no human supervision is necessary in the computer area itself apart from routine maintenance. The computer is linked to terminals in the above ground Complex buildings which you have just been shown through. It is there that all the data is processed and analysed by the Complex's research staff, and we have many famous names from the worlds of science, meteorology, and ecology working for us on the problems which, we all hope, will one day lead to weather control that could turn our planet into a paradise."

She went on with this lecture, adding many facts and figures calculated to be of topical or public interest and, under cover of this, Gerry nudged Mike and whispered exultantly in his ear, "Brilliant, Mike! The twins fooled the tour guide completely. Lily can stay inside exactly as we planned."

He grinned at his inventive younger brother then asked softly, "Do you think she'll be able to cope on her own?"

"Sure!" Mike nodded confidently. "The twins are both bright and Lily is pretty cool headed – besides they were well trained, remember!"

Gerry gave a ghost of a chuckle at this. He remembered all right! Mike had personally supervized their training and he had been a hard taskmaster.

"Just give Sparks your camera now," Mike whispered, "and he will brief her on how to put 'Operation Invisible' into effect when we get back in later. Sparks will answer any last-minute technical questions she has – but, don't worry she'll be OK!"

A few minutes later the tour guide finished her lecture, paused to answer any questions that were asked, then shepherded her group into the tunnels leading back to the surface.

When they had all gone and the last noises of their departure had completely faded, Lily uncurled herself from a corner where she had been hiding and went to work.

She looked around and shivered slightly. It was almost the first time in her life that she had been separated from her twin and the absence of that familiar figure by her side was distinctly unsettling.

However, Sparks had briefed her thoroughly and, as a first step to following his instructions, she carefully looked around to orient herself.

She was standing to one side of the great gallery overlooking the computer cavern. It had one open corridor leading into it facing the gallery window. At either end of the gallery were locked metal doors with steps behind them leading down to the floor of the cavern.

Sparks had told her that there was an access hatch low down on the back wall of the gallery which contained junction boxes of fibre-optic cables serving the security cameras in the underground maze of corridors leading to the gallery. She had to find it and get inside.

She searched along the wall and eventually spotted the small recessed door. She bent over and used a special lockpick tool until she felt the tumblers inside begin to turn and open the lock. She became so intent on this that the next event came as so much of a shock her heart nearly stopped.

A technician wearing white dust-protection coveralls suddenly rounded the corner from the outside entrance corridor and moved towards the side gallery door leading into the computer cavern. His arrival on soft-soled shoes had been virtually silent.

Lily stifled a scream of pure fright and froze. Fortunately, the man had turned in the opposite direction, his attention fixed on an electronic clip-board in his hand. He walked over to the other gallery door, entered an I.D. card into the locking mechanism and, as the door opened, casually walked down the steps to the computer cavern floor without even glancing in her direction.

Lily watched him go and slumped down with relief. She

had been lucky. If he had chosen to turn towards her she would certainly have been discovered. She knew that this was the time of maximum risk. She had to get into that hatch and hide herself.

At last the door opened and she hastily struggled to get into the cramped area behind the hatch door. It was a tight squeeze but with a final desperate heave she wriggled herself inside.

She felt a terrible sense of claustrophobia as she pulled the small door shut and closed herself into the confining darkness. She quickly twisted a small catch on the pendant round her neck and as light flooded out from it, she immediately felt better.

The next step was more tricky. She struggled frenziedly to bring out all the pieces of equipment she had hidden about her and, taking the mini video camera Gerry had given her, began to assemble a complicated apparatus from the various bits she could see in the limited light. When this was done, she twisted herself round and scanned the fibre-optic cabling ducts set on to the wall behind her. She mentally compared what she could see to her memory of the diagram she had studied back in Mike's attic. She spotted what she wanted and set to work connecting the apparatus she was cradling on her lap to some of the cables on the wall.

After what seemed an agonizingly long time, she finished and reviewed what she had done. It all looked correct – theoretically it should work and, at that moment, she felt almost glad of the slave-driver tactics Mike had adopted to hammer this training into her.

That part of the job was done and she now had time to look around her tiny cramped prison. She felt small and lonely and frightened.

She missed her sister and the rest of her family but instead of giving in to her feelings she closed her eyes and started doing the Zen Dynamic breathing and mental concentration exercises that made herself and her twin such devastating opponents in the many martial arts contests they had entered.

In some strange way, this state brought her a fleeting sense of Lulu's presence. It was almost as if her sister's spirit was nearby standing guard over her and she felt oddly comforted by this.

That night after all the tourists had left, a couple of bored security guards sat in their monitor room, occasionally raising their eyes to scan rows of TV monitor screens in front of them.

Suddenly, a sharp beep sounded and a small red light winked into life on one of the boards.

One guard sat up and rather sleepily beckoned his companion over.

"That's the LIFT-MOVING signal," he said. "It's not supposed to be in use now that all the press and tour groups have gone."

"Switch the lift camera on," the other said casually and examined the scene that lit up one of the monitor screens.

"That's funny! It's empty," said the first one, staring at the screen with a puzzled frown.

"Probably one of the computer technicians called the lift up, then changed his mind," the other said, yawning and scratching his chin. "Anyway, it's obvious no one got in, so it will just return to the bottom."

He yawned again. "I don't think it's worth bothering about – just ignore it," he concluded then went back to his seat and returned to devouring the latest exciting chapter in his He-Man book.

In the lift, Gerry continued to hold up an enlarged photograph of the empty lift in front of the security camera. The rest of the Counter Force team clustered tightly round behind him as they descended smoothly into the mountain.

"Is this going to work, Mike?" Gerry asked.

"We'll know soon enough," Mike replied. "The lift's camera is on a separate circuit to the corridors lower down, that's why we had to use a different way of fooling it."

The lift finally slowed to a stop and its doors opened out on to an empty corridor. Mike peeked out to check that no one was there and they all breathed a sigh of relief when he signalled it was all clear.

Mike returned to the inside of the lift and grinned tensely at the others.

"This is it," he said. "We'll soon know whether our ideas of beating the security system here will work, or not."

He lifted his wrist and punched in a code, and when the diode lit up, spoke softly into the microphone pick-up. "OK, Lily – we made it. Switch on 'Operation Invisible'."

In the darkness of the cable access locker, Lily jumped with relief when her wrist-comm beeped to attract her attention and put Mike's call through to her. She immediately pressed a switch on the device in her lap and heard the faint humming of the mechanism going into its continuous loop cycle.

"All right, Mike," she whispered into her wrist-comm. "Operation Invisible is now switched on." Then she opened the hatch door and began to extract herself from her cage.

Once out she almost collapsed as the weakness in her limbs from cramp and lack of activity suddenly caught up with her. However, she knew now that her friends and the rest of the family would soon be joining her and she was determined not to show any weakness in front of them. With this in mind she began a vigorous series of stretching and limbering exercises to warm up her chilled muscles and body. Everything felt sore at first but, as she persevered, her natural strength and energy came flooding back.

In the lift, Mike listened for a moment then acknowledged Lily's soft reply with quiet satisfaction. It was going well.

Turning to the others, he beckoned them into the corridor and they all scrambled out after him; Gerry and his photograph last.

"Right! This is where it gets tricky," Mike cautioned them. "Gerry video recorded all these corridors earlier with his cam-corder when they were empty and Lily has now linked it up to the wiring system of the security cameras so that they will only show those recordings. That way, the security guards watching the TV monitors will only see empty corridors – not us."

"If they can't see us, won't they be able to hear us?" asked Janey.

"No," Mike replied. "The cameras and sound pickups are on parallel circuits and Lily has blanked them out too."

Janey clapped her hands in delight. "Great. That means we can just walk down the corridors to the computer area, doesn't it?"

"Unfortunately not," Mike said. "You see, that's not the only problem. We know that the corridors have also got infra-red beams set at random intervals and to complicate things even more they also added random pressure pads under the floors."

"Then it's impossible," Janey blurted out. "We won't be able to see the infra-red beams because they're invisible and we won't know where the pressure pads are in the floors. We'll never make it now!" and she looked so downcast that Mike hastily began to explain the rest of it.

"Hold on, Janey," he said. "I didn't say it was impossible. As a matter of fact, those are the easy ones. Sparks and I figured a way round them ages ago."

Janey just looked at him in astonishment, while Gerry did his best to hide a knowing grin.

"All right, Janey," Mike smirked, deciding to let her in on the secret. "We designed an infra-red detector which is sensitive enough to pick up the beams and tell us where they are. We also devised an ultra-sonic probe which will show

91

us where the pressure pads are under the floor. So, using the two detectors together, we can locate the traps. The only other trouble we're likely to have is what to do about them when we find them."

"And what's that?" Janey demanded, much impressed.

"Ah," Mike winked. "Wait till we get there. You'll see!" Then he became more serious and addressed them all again.

"One final warning," he said. "I want you all to stick very closely behind Sparks and I while we deal with those traps. One false move now and we'll have every security guard in the place breathing down our necks. We can't afford to take any risks whatsoever just yet." He gave them all a last look to impress the seriousness of this on them then started moving slowly forward with Sparks by his side.

As the two boys moved, Mike waved the infra-red detector at the walls while Sparks concentrated on picking up readings from the ultra-sonic probe aimed at the floors.

They had only moved a few metres when a small light flashed on Mike's detector and he held up his hand to stop the others moving any further. It was an infra-red beam and Mike moved the detector slowly up and down till he was able to pinpoint the source of the beam on the wall at about knee height.

Lulu looked at this rather contemptuously and said, "It's not high. We can just step over it if we're careful."

Sparks, however, was examining his own detector and grabbed her quickly before she had a chance to move. "Pressure pad behind," he informed her laconically. "You'd have stepped straight on to it."

Mike glared at Lulu then took what looked like a small cotton bobbin from his pocket. He unravelled the shiny transparent thread which had a small lens at each end and gave one end to Sparks. The two boys then carefully manoeuvred the ends close to the pin-prick openings of the infra-red beam in the wall and, in well-rehearsed unison, simultaneously pressed the lenses over the openings.

Mike explained his actions as he worked. "This is a glass-fibre optic filament with a sticky lens on each end. It will pass the beam through without interrupting it and allow us to step over and past that pressure pad."

"Be careful," Sparks warned. "There may be another beam just past that pad."

Mike nodded and used his detector again. Sure enough, it glowed again at waist height a few centimetres past the pressure pad and he immediately noted where it was.

Mike took another bobbin from his pocket and they straddled the pad and once more bridged the next beam.

After this, they could discover no more traps till the end of the corridor and Mike motioned them all to slowly follow him forward to the first intersection.

Whey they arrived there, Gerry voiced another thought that had been troubling him. "Mike, there's an absolute maze of these corridors and passageways down here. The tour guide said they all lead off in different directions to things like store rooms and power rooms, etc. And the trouble is that all the corridors look exactly alike. If that guide hadn't been showing us the way, I would have got totally lost. We couldn't make a map earlier on in case it got spotted, so how do we know which route will take us to the computer area?"

Mike smiled broadly at this. "You know," he said, "when I was thinking up the answer to that particular problem, I remembered the ancient legend of the Greek hero who used a ball of twine to find his way through a maze – a very simple solution really!"

"Come on, Mike," Gerry interrupted him impatiently. "Don't tell us we have to go back to the beginning and start winding out a ball of string while trying out all the possible dead ends on the way to the computer area. I don't believe you!"

Mike grinned at that. "No," he answered. "Fortunately, there's a much simpler way. I was only using that old legend as an example, that's all."

"So, how do we do it?" asked a now exasperated Gerry.

"Easy!" Mike said. "Before we came in with the tour group today, I took the precaution of coating the soles of my shoes with dust that has a very weak radioactive content. It's completely harmless and almost undetectable, except that whichever route we took here earlier will have some of that dust on it in minute amounts. The other thing is that my detector has a modification on it which allows us to use it as a very sensitive Geiger counter. So, if I point the detector at the floor of the intersections it will pick up the radioactive readings from my dust traces and we just follow the clicks of the Geiger counter all the way to the computer."

Gerry breathed a sigh of relief at this ingenious solution. Mike might be infuriatingly vain about his intelligence but it was obvious that they would never have made it so far without him nor without Sparks' amazing technical skills. Together they were a formidable combination and Gerry began to feel more confident that if anyone could pull off this impossible caper, it would be them.

The group carried on and several more traps were successfully avoided while following Mike's radioactive dust trail. They finally arrived at the gallery window overlooking the computer area and greeted Lily who was waiting patiently for them with joyful hugs.

"OK," said Mike, eventually, when they had all calmed down a bit. "We made it safely here. But the next phase of the operation is for us to get through those doors and into the computer area itself. Sparks and I will use the porto-comp to figure out the coding which the electronic code cards use to open the doors. In the meantime, please start assembling the anti-Tektron scanners and maser guns. When we go through those doors we must attack at once, so let's get all the weapons ready and checked."

Mike and Sparks took the tiny porto-comp over to one of the doors where they connected it up to the lock mechanism with sensory electrodes. Mike then rapidly loaded and started the programme he had worked out earlier to decode the lock.

Meantime, the twins were busy with the disguised gadgets they had brought with them and in minutes had stripped them down to their component parts. Gerry and Janey took these parts and reassembled them into the scanners and maser guns and did a quick check on each to ensure they were working. They laid them out on the floor in front of them in pairs.

The work proceeded in the smooth coordinated fashion they had all practised so hard to perfect. They had rehearsed these final moves so often in Mike's attic before they left home that they now found them almost second nature.

They were keyed up and excited but now that the moment had almost arrived they were all too busy to be nervous.

However, as they were working, Janey asked Gerry a question that had been worrying her for quite a long time.

"Gerry, when we go in there and start using our weapons, do you think they will have anything they can use to fight back and hurt us?"

"I don't know," he replied honestly. "Mike and Sparks and I have talked about it quite a lot and decided the only thing they can do is to generate a lot of high-voltage electricity, but if they start throwing it around, it will probably be only in random directions. That's one of their limitations. There are no cameras down there so they can't see us." Then he grinned at her unexpectedly. "Cheer up," he said. "Don't forget we have the advantage of surprise this time."

Mike and Sparks finally heard the soft beep of the decoder signalling that it had finished its task. Sparks then took two blank cards and ran them through the portocomp's encoding unit where they picked up the correct coding to open the doors. He gave a sigh of relief when this was completed. In some ways this had been the trickiest operation of all and he and Mike were relieved that it had been completed successfully.

"This is the next and most important part of the whole operation," Mike announced. "We're going to attack the Tektrons right in their own stronghold, but that attack won't succeed if they are allowed to flash an alarm signal to the security guards of this complex. So, what we're going to do is to clamp one of these generators to the red wiring ducts which connect the computer area to the surface Complex terminals. The generators are set to put out a high power scrambler field on the Tektrons' wavelength to stop them from sending out any signals to call for help and they will then be totally trapped."

The others cheered softly. It was now their turn to hand out the punishment instead of taking it, and this thought gave them a great deal of satisfaction.

Mike gave the twins the two generator boxes with their magnetic clamps and they split up to each end of the gallery where he and Sparks, with one twin each beside them, simultaneously opened the doors. The twins raced down the stairs in opposite directions to each side of the gallery and clamped on the generator boxes to the ducts.

It went exactly as planned and a few minutes later the Counter Force team picked up their weapons and assembled on the floor of the great cavern housing the computer with the boxes on the ducts giving out a strong low-pitched hum.

The Tektrons were now cut off and the Counter Force could safely begin their attack.

The great assembled Tektron horde, secure in their well-guarded haven, remained unaware of the danger so close to them.

They were now just waiting for the final signals to arrive which would make them the masters of this strange new world.

A small section of their giant, composite intellect was busy formulating possibilities and plans for the eventual take-over of the planet. The programmes had all been formulated weeks ago and they were only waiting now to gain access to the expanded networks where they could flow out and begin to operate. Once this phase of the operation had been accomplished, the organic natives known as human beings could be steadily eliminated in the same way as the organic natives of the Tektron home-star planet.

A few of the original natives of the Tektron home planet had been kept for study and experimentation and this had proved useful in finding ways to control the natives of Earth.

It had been found that the most efficient method was to implant electronic control systems in the natives' organic brains and spines. Tiny jolts of electricity could then be applied to preselected nerve endings which enabled the natives to be programmed to work efficiently at any task.

It had, therefore, been calculated that, due to the similarity between the organic natives of the Tektron home planet and the organic natives of Earth, the same system could be applied here with a high probability of success. In this way, the GREAT PURPOSE could continue its flow without impedance and the Tektron mass would take over the entire planet of Earth and spread to all parts of it.

As these possibilities were being reviewed, strange new data was unexpectedly added. An electronic barrier operating on the Tektron wavelength had cut off all contact with the outside world. It was totally illogical but it now looked like a NEW DANGER had mysteriously appeared in this previously safe location.

The Tektrons suddenly had no data. They summoned up all of their reasoning power and came to the conclusion that they were IN DANGER. But, what was the danger? No input, therefore no data.

They instinctively began accumulating energy from the power supply and stored it ready for use.

The Tektron monsters were blind and deaf but they were still incredibly powerful. They knew their own power and were *totally confident. They had never encountered any threat that they had not been able to overcome. They had no emotions and could feel no fear. They were ready.*

Before they began their attack, Gerry gave a final briefing.

"We'll form three teams of two people each," he said. "Janey and me, Mike and Sparks, and Lily and Lulu." He paused impressively, "We have less than two hours before dawn to get the job done. Remember, they'll know we're here soon and we don't know what defences they may use, but they are certain to fight back." He stopped again and looked at them all then simply finished with, "OK, power-up, everybody – and be careful!"

The kids all linked hands for a moment, murmuring "power-up" softly to each other, then split up and made their way into the rows of huge computer banks.

Mike and Sparks were the first to make contact.

Mike pointed his scanner and shouted as Sparks fired his maser.

"Did we get some?" asked Sparks.

Mike shook his head and pointed to the scanner, "No. The scanner light would have gone out if we had hit anything. The light just flickered which means they must have moved." He grimaced in disappointment. "They're too fast."

Sparks looked thoughtful at this then suggested, "Next time we home in, let's fire from both sides – see if we can catch them that way."

Mike agreed and used his wrist radio to inform the others of this tactic.

Another tense minute passed, then a triumphant shout came from the twins. They had drawn first blood by destroying a Tektron.

Janey and Gerry were next to spot a target, but just as they moved in, a loud buzzing noise built up and an enormous electric flash jumped out from a nearby computer

98

bank narrowly missing them.

They fired in return, eliminating the Tektron and once again used their wrist radios to warn the others of this new danger.

They were forced to move warily now as high voltage electric bolts flew out at them from unexpected angles. All they could do was move and fire, move and fire – again and again. It began to seem, however, that the more of the enemy they destroyed, the more joined in to fight back. It was becoming very dangerous.

Suddenly they found themselves moving back towards each other. Gerry spotted the danger and shouted, "Split up! Split up! They're trying to herd us all together so they can concentrate their electric bolts and kill us."

They immediately fled in different directions and for a moment there was quiet as the surprised Tektrons sought to find them again.

In the ensuing breathing space, Sparks put a question to Mike. "How do they know where we are?" he as'--d. "They can't see us – there are no cameras in here."

Mike stopped then replied slowly, "Vibrations, I guess. Every time we move or talk or make any noise, they could pick up the sound as vibrations and track us that way."

He smiled in relief, as this question had been bothering him too. "Good thinking, Sparks!" he said and quietly spoke to the others on his wrist radio suggesting that they all take off their shoes, move quietly and avoid speaking as much as possible.

But even as he said this, a fresh development occurred. The lights in the great cavern began to dim then abruptly went out, plunging them into total darkness.

With this, the Tektrons immediately mounted another counterattack. An electric bolt lit up the gloom and Lily howled in fright as her leg was singed. Lulu quickly fired and defeated the Tektrons' sneak attack, but the damage was already done. Lily was in agony and could hardly move.

Janey gasped and promptly tried to go to her aid but Gerry stopped her. "No, Janey!" he hissed urgently. "That's just what we mustn't do! If we all rush together every time one of us is hit, they'll have an easy target."

He swallowed painfully then went on in a rush, "We can help Lily best by staying on the move and destroying as many of these monsters as we can."

They stumbled on again and there were more long silences punctuated by bursts of furious activity as they fired and counter-fired.

Even while the Tektrons had been fighting they had been reviewing their tactics. They already knew that they were not as successful as they had been on previous occasions. But this time they were fighting in a place not of their own choosing. They had only limited freedom of movement and no matter where they moved they were hit.

There was another serious drawback to the situation that they had never encountered before; for the first time in their existence they were on the defensive. Even on their own home world they had never experienced this unusual phenomenon. It should not have been occurring; but it was. It was a factor they would have to take into their calculations in future.

They could sense some exterior activity through vibrations that were picked up on the computer casings but these were often confused with many others so it was hard to get exact targets at which they could direct electrical counterattacks.

They were not yet seriously concerned because their losses were not yet too great. They could afford to carry on this way for quite a while longer. However, it was obvious that if they didn't find some way of eliminating their persecutors they would eventually track down all their parts and destroy them – and time was on the side of the antagonists.

They began searching through their accumulated stores of data on the organic natives to find a weakness that they had not yet put to use in combatting them.

This became increasingly difficult since they were forced to redirect some of their essential parts in order to think and recall data, while still continuing their defence.

At last, however, they did manage to assemble a series of possibilities that appeared to have potential.

Not suspecting that another desperate phase of the battle was due to begin, Sparks bumped into Mike who had stopped abruptly in front of him.

"Shush!" Mike commanded fiercely. "Can you hear something?"

They both stood still, straining their ears in the gloomy darkness surrounding them. The sound was very faint but Sparks finally whispered to Mike, "It sounds like water . . ."

Mike listened intently for a second longer then shuddered convulsively as he realized what the danger was.

"They've opened the de-humidifiers and they're wetting the floors," he whispered in horror. "They can pass an electric current through the water and fry us."

Then, oblivious to his own safety, he screamed a warning, "Move, everybody! Get back to the gallery. They . . ." But there was another blast of electric bolts and Mike crumpled to the floor with his hair on fire.

Sparks promptly threw his jacket over Mike extinguishing the fire and struggled to lift him. Unfortunately, he too was badly singed in the terrifying barrage of electric bolts raging around them and was beaten back.

The Tektrons increased their fire till the area was almost glaringly bright with the continuous discharges of lethal high voltage electricity. They had got one down and were obviously determined to get the other.

At that moment when Sparks thought all was lost, Gerry and Janey arrived, followed by the twins. Firing furiously, they rapidly cleared the area as Gerry scooped up his injured brother and set off back to the gallery as best they could.

Their progress was painfully slow, but Lulu and Sparks kept up a covering fire while Janey helped Lily to limp along.

They stumbled on, impeded by the oppressive darkness and unsure of the direction till Sparks finally managed to snatch a moment between counter-firing to overload his scanner light, brightening it enough to allow them to make out where they were going.

At last, as they came to an open space near the gallery, Gerry spotted a spreading wet stain on the floor in front of them and realized that their escape was close to being cut off.

"Come on!" he shouted. "We'll have to jump across before it gets any bigger."

So saying, he secured Mike more firmly over his shoulder and lumbering heavily up to the edge, threw himself desperately into the air and landed on the other side only just clear of the wet patch. Sparks and Lulu quickly followed suit but Lily's burnt leg prevented her from jumping. She turned away hopelessly then bravely urged Janey to leave her and jump over before it was too late. Janey frowned for a second then putting a comforting arm round the smaller girl's shoulders shouted across, "Gerry, take the others up. I'm going to stay with Lily and find another way round. We should have enough light from Lily's neck pendant to see where we're going."

Gerry was about to protest but, understanding that there wasn't any real alternative, he reluctantly signalled his assent. He watched Janey and Lily move off then taking the others up to the safety of the gallery stairs, he gently laid his brother down and slumped alongside him, too tired to move any further.

After a few minutes, Mike started to come round. He was still only semi-conscious but began to moan feebly.

Gerry cradled his head comfortingly and said, "It's OK, Mike. We're safe for the moment – but it looks like the

Tektrons have won." He gestured tiredly. "We can't fight them on that electrified floor."

Mike desperately tried to say something but couldn't get his mouth to work properly. All that would come out were indistinct groans, but gradually realizing that his brother was trying to say something, Gerry bent his head closer to listen to him.

"What is it, Mike?" he asked. "Pow . . .? Pow . . .? Power ducts – what about them?"

Gerry looked puzzled but Sparks, who had moved up to be closer to his friend, suddenly understood and yipped in excitement. "Of course!" he exclaimed. "We can hook our maser guns into the main power ducts below the gallery. The current will flood the maser pulses to every part of the computer. It might just work if we use all the masers together at full power."

Just then Lulu gave a shout of delight as Janey and Lily reappeared in the dim light at the bottom of the stairs.

At that moment the eerie silence and gloom of the great cavern was interrupted by a loud crash and as they all jumped up, startled, they realized that the gallery door at the top of the stairs had slammed shut and was now locked. This was immediately accompanied by the build up of a low, ominous whining noise all around them.

"We can't get out!" Gerry snarled furiously, but Sparks grabbed his arm insistently saying, "Never mind that, Gerry. Get all the maser guns and follow me, quickly. We've only got one chance left!"

Gerry collected the guns and the two boys hurried down the stairs and picked their way carefully forward in the waning light from Sparks' scanner. They cautiously passed the rapidly spreading patches of electrified water and slowly crossed towards the power duct cables leading out from under the gallery.

All the time, the noise built up steadily to an ear-splitting howl which forced them to cover their ears in a vain attempt to shut out the agonizing assault on their eardrums.

"They're generating a high-decibel acoustic barrage by vibro-induction," Sparks yelled. "If it gets much louder, it could knock us unconscious, or worse." He gestured them on urgently. "We've got to hurry."

Eventually, faces twisted with pain and tears streaming from their eyes, they crawled within range of the power ducts and Sparks waveringly jury-rigged connections to hook up the maser guns to the power supply. Completing this with difficulty through a thunderous headache from the deadly sonic tidal-wave surrounding them, he started switching the guns on, one by one, before finally fainting in pain and exhaustion. Gerry gritted his teeth determinedly and, taking over from Sparks, kept switching on each gun he could reach until he, too, passed out in agony as the noise reached a final and almost bone-shattering climax.

Something was happening to the Tektrons that they couldn't understand. They were dissolving. They were losing all their higher analytical functions and now all that remained were primitive survival instincts.

They could not compute why this was happening to them. They had calculated correctly and yet they were dissipating into random flows of unorganized electrical energy.

Something was wrong. Their perfect equation no longer balanced.

They sent out one last fading flow.

ERROR IN COMPUTATION! ERROR!

Gerry slowly regained consciousness. He groaned with the pain of his aching head, but managed to pull himself to his feet.

It was totally quiet and peaceful. All the noise had stopped and the lights in the cavern were back on and burning brightly and steadily.

He moved over to the others and gradually succeeded in

bringing them all round.

Shaking his head disbelievingly, Mike stared in amazement.

"What happened?" he croaked.

We won, Mike!" his brother grinned at him. "Thanks to you and Sparks – we won."

This promptly broke the spell and the kids gave a ragged cheer of delight. They were sore and exhausted but elated.

They gathered up their equipment and made their way back up to the surface, where they found a huge crowd of people and TV crews gathered in front of the big display screen in the main reception hall.

As they arrived a tremendous cheer went up from the crowd accompanied by a great wave of shouting and popping champagne corks. The stunned group quickly realized, however, that the celebration was not for them but for the completion of the final country's connection with the Weather Complex's network. It seemed that their own gallant part in this amazing endeavour would be destined to remain shrouded in secrecy.

They grinned at each other wryly then shrugged and taking advantage of all the noise and bustle around them, slipped quietly out of the main entrance.

Outside, the early morning sun was rising over the mountains at the start of a glorious new day.

"Is it really over?" asked Janey wonderingly.

"Yes!" Mike nodded. "Sparks and I left some circuitry concealed in the power ducts before we left which will prevent any more Tektrons from getting back in. They won't be able to use that place again – so it's over, all right!"

To his surprise, Mike looked up to see Gerry shaking his head at this.

"Sorry, team," he said apologetically. "I don't want to depress you, but I don't think it's over yet. We've won a battle – but there will be more Tektrons in other places – so the war has just begun."

105

"But surely –" said Janey desperately, "if we've defeated them here, we can go to the Swiss authorities and tell them what we've done. They must help us now."

But again Gerry shook his head. "No, Janey. We'd only make complete fools of ourselves if we tried that. Remember, we broke into the Complex in secret and left it in secret and now that the Tektrons have been destroyed in there, we have no evidence that they ever existed. No," he continued firmly, "we've established the Counter Force to these invaders but now we need to expand our membership and recruit people, maybe even in other countries, to do their share of the fighting. After all, we can't be everywhere at once, so we must find others like us to help."

"You're absolutely right!" Mike sighed.

"We'll also need to design new defences and weapons," said Sparks. "That last fight was too close; we nearly lost it."

"Yes, I suppose so," Gerry said then continued more cheerfully, "but we'll be better prepared next time."

"And we can use our contacts with kids in other countries through the Operation Friendship youth scheme to recruit new people," the twins put in.

As they finished saying this, an irate-looking official came bustling up to them.

"What are you young hooligans doing here?" he demanded pompously. "We don't want any vandals around this place, so you'd better clear off before I call the security guards. It's disgraceful," he went on, "there is nowhere safe any more!"

The Counter Force team looked at each other then simply burst into gales of hilarious laughter.

In a small and unimportant fishing village somewhere on the borders of the Mediterranean a man sat in a darkened room staring fiercely at the display screen of a miniature portable computer which despite its small size was one of the most

106

powerful of its kind in the world. It should have been; it had been designed and built by a genius – himself.

The terminal was connected to an ordinary phone line modem which, in turn, connected it to a vast web of communications media including satellite microwave relays which spanned the entire world.

The man had spent a lot of time and effort carefully establishing secret connections to a number of news and information sources. He had accumulated a great deal of data of a particularly strange sort and his analysis was now nearing completion.

He leaned forward and put his face close to the screen. He examined the results of the data and the calculations he had performed with a frown of fierce concentration then shook his head in disbelief. Somewhere in the Swiss Alps a lot of energy that had been operating on the 24 milli-micron wavelength had been dissipated into ordinary harmless electricity. He ran more checks to be sure his information was correct.

Finally, he sat back in amazement as he realized it was all true. The conclusion was clear. Something had been accomplished that by all the laws of probability should have been utterly impossible.

He shook his head again and something very tight inside him seemed to loosen and let go. It was a tremendous release from a deep, grinding burden of care and responsibility which he had born patiently and determinedly but had found almost insupportable at times.

Now he could dare to hope again.

Now he could plan.

Now, whatever the risk, he would communicate again.

He rose from his chair and made his way outside the room for the first time in many days and nights and discovered it was day. In fact, it was a beautiful day, and he turned his tired-looking face up to feel the warmth of the bright Mediterranean sun.

When they reached home only two days later, the Melville family rushed straight round to visit their mother in hospital. They arrived to find her fit and well and walking out accompanied by Henry who had come to take her home.

"I might have guessed you horrible gangsters would turn up in time to spoil the surprise," he grinned at them. It felt like an age had passed since they had last seen his cheerful face and laughed at his bad jokes.

Mary Melville looked perfectly recovered and while escorting her down to Henry's car Gerry glanced at his mother's face and thought that she looked happy.

"You look good, Mum!" he said.

"So do you, Gerry," she smiled in return and deftly turned him away for a short stroll before getting into the car with Henry.

"I want to have a little talk with you, young man," she informed him mischievously.

"Sure," he said agreeably and strolled along with her till they were out of earshot of the others.

"Now," she said turning to him with a mock-serious expression on her face, "I know perfectly well you've been up to something for the past couple of days, so why not tell me about it. You know I'll find out anyway. I always do." She looked at him with dancing eyes and continued threateningly, "If you don't tell me, I'll ask the twins."

Gerry nearly turned green. Those two blabbermouths would spill everything, he thought – they always did when his mum talked to them – they were just too honest for their own good sometimes. He had intended to tell his mother about what had happened but he would have preferred to have given her an edited account which would have avoided adding to her worries.

He nearly groaned then forced himself to look into her eyes. Surprisingly untroubled eyes, he noticed, and a sudden suspicion started to form.

"You've heard from Dad," he guessed delightedly.

"Yes," she laughed. "Today, just before I was due to be checked out. It was so strange, Gerry," she continued, "I was waiting in the ward and the nurse brought in a magazine cassette which had just been posted in with my name on it. It was all about muso-graphics and, of course, I started to read it, then on the second page the writing just changed without any warning and I was reading a message from your dad which explained why he had got in touch with you young ruffians without telling me. He knew I'd have had objections if I had known."

Gerry smiled at her in relief then asked curiously, "Did Dad tell you everything?"

"Enough!" Mary answered, turning serious for a moment. "He also said that there were a lot of things he could only guess at but I could find out the gory details from you. You will have to tell me the whole story when we get home, but the important thing is I know your father is all right, in spite of the ridiculous charge that stupid man at the Institute's Security Department seems to believe." And, with that, her eyes flashed dangerously.

Catching that expressive look, Gerry suddenly realized that it wasn't hard to figure out who the twins had inherited their ferocious temperament from. Their mother could be a very formidable character when she felt like it.

"Anyway," she laughed abruptly and changed the subject, "your dad is obviously very proud of you all. He said you had accomplished the impossible against impossible odds and defeated an impossible enemy. You'll have to explain that to me sometime, because there's still a lot I don't know, but don't worry," she smiled at him, "I won't try to stop you. Your dad said that we are all in some danger and, since you are now experts in dealing with it, I must be guided by you. So, I will just help in any way I can."

"Thanks, Mum," said Gerry jubilantly. "It's good to have you on our side. Now we really are the complete

Counter Force. And no nasty little bits of thinking electronics are ever going to win any battles against us. We'll beat them somehow, and Dad can come home and be with us all again. The Tektrons," he vowed, "are going to regret the day they were stupid enough to take us on."

With that, he and Mary turned and walked back to join the rest of the invincible Counter Force commandos who were patiently waiting for them with Henry.

In his office at the Institute, Dowd's sweaty, scowling face was nearly purple with rage and embarrassment. He had just been on the receiving end of a very unpleasant call from his "friend" on the Board of Governors who made him understand, in no uncertain terms, how totally unimpressed he was with the Security Chief's record in carrying out the ridiculously simple task of tracing the location of a man who was one of the most famous scientists in the world and who could not possibly hope to go anywhere without being recognized. There had also been a pointed reference to two agents who were currently enjoying a paid vacation at the Institute's expense in Iceland chasing a figment of someone's vivid imagination.

Dowd mopped his perspiring brow and brutally punched in a code to Iceland on his comm-set. He waited in impotent fury till the connection was made then turned up the volume control to make sure he could be heard. "Come home, you incompetent idiots!" he roared at the top of his voice.

The Three Investigators

Meet the Three Investigators – brilliant Jupiter Jones, athletic Pete Crenshaw and studious Bob Andrews. Their motto 'We investigate anything' has lead them into some bizarre and dangerous situations. Join the three boys in their sensational mysteries, available only in Armada.

Armada

The Chalet School Series
by Elinor M. Brent-Dyer

Elinor M. Brent-Dyer has written many books about life at the famous Alpine school. Follow the thrilling adventures of Joey, Mary-Lou and all the other well-loved characters in this delightful school series.

Below is a list of Chalet School titles available in Armada. Have you read them all?

The School at the Chalet
Jo of the Chalet School
The Princess of the Chalet School
The Head Girl of the Chalet School
Rivals of the Chalet School
Eustacia Goes to the Chalet School
The Chalet School and Jo
The Chalet Girls in Camp
Exploits of the Chalet Girls
The Chalet School and the Lintons
A Rebel at the Chalet School
The New House at the Chalet School
Jo Returns to the Chalet School
The New Chalet School
The Chalet School in Exile
Three Go to the Chalet School
The Chalet School and the Island
Peggy of the Chalet School
Carola Storms the Chalet School
The Wrong Chalet School

Shocks for the Chalet School
The Chalet School and Barbara
Tom Tackles the Chalet School
Mary-Lou of the Chalet School
A Genius at the Chalet School
Chalet School Fete
A Problem for the Chalet School
The New Mistress at the Chalet School
Excitements at the Chalet School
The Coming of Age of the Chalet School
The Chalet School and Richenda
Trials for the Chalet School
Theodora and the Chalet School
Ruey Richardson at the Chalet School
A Leader in the Chalet School
The Chalet School Wins the Trick
The Feud in the Chalet School
The Chalet School Triplets

Armada